Moonlight glinted off his angry eyes

"*You* again!" Rosalba addressed the dark stranger, feeling confused but not surprised. "You are like a hawk, *signore*, always hovering. Are you my self-elected protector?"

"A hawk does not protect, *signorina*," he told her in a flat monotone that nevertheless managed to convey inward furor. "Its function is to hunt, to pounce and then to destroy."

Though the night was balmy, Rosalba shuddered. There was menace in his tone and a contempt she found somehow threatening. "Why are you so interested in my movements? D-don't deny that you are," she stumbled over her words in anxious haste. "Why me?"

He laughed a harsh mirthless laugh. "Because you are the most important person in the world to me. You shall be the instrument of a fate long overdue."

MARGARET ROME
is also the author of these

Harlequin Presents

and these

Harlequin Romances

Many of these titles are available at your local bookseller.

For a free catalogue listing all available Harlequin Romances
and Harlequin Presents, send your name and address to:

HARLEQUIN READER SERVICE
1440 South Priest Drive, Tempe, AZ 85281
Canadian address: Stratford, Ontario N5A 6W2

MARGARET ROME

castle of the fountains

Harlequin Books

TORONTO • LONDON • LOS ANGELES • AMSTERDAM
SYDNEY • HAMBURG • PARIS • STOCKHOLM • ATHENS • TOKYO

Harlequin Presents first edition September 1982
ISBN 0-373-10532-0

Original hardcover edition published in 1979
by Mills & Boon Limited

CHAPTER ONE

'ROSALBA, why don't you come with me to Città del Monte?'

The instant the impulsive words were uttered Aprile wanted to retract them. But predictably, at the mere suggestion of doing anything out of the ordinary, her cousin Rosalba's eyes grew round with apprehension, her lips hastily framed a stammered refusal.

'Oh, no, thank you, Aprile, I couldn't possibly.'

Perversely, although she had already decided that in her saner moments the last companion she would have chosen to accompany her on her annual, much-looked-forward-to holiday in Sicily was her meek, unassuming cousin, Aprile fixed Rosalba with a hard stare and demanded:

'Why not, for heaven's sake? You never go anywhere, you never *do* anything—and besides that,' she stressed, 'Nonno Rossi has expressed a wish that you should visit him.' She waited for Rosalba's reaction, shamefacedly admitting to herself that the invitation had been motivated not by a desire for her cousin's company but because of the silken stress their aged yet still domineering grandfather had placed upon his words just before she had last taken leave of him.

They had been sitting together in the back of his chauffeur-driven limousine awaiting the arrival at

Palermo airport of the plane that was about to carry her away from the luxury of his patronage—from the exciting social whirl that began the moment they took up residence in his house in the capital; from glorious sun-soaked days spent in his villa by the sea; from his palatial family seat, a castle high upon a mountain that was approached by a road lined with miles upon miles of vineyards, roads upon which lorries rumbled piled high with grapes destined for the winery where they would be pressed, processed, and the juice finally poured into bottles labelled with the family crest.

Back to what? Moodily Aprile had stared out of the window. Back to a boring office job in rain-soaked northern England, to dull routine, to penny-pinching, to a type of existence, in fact, that was totally unsuited to the granddaughter of the Conte Piero Rossi di Città del Monte.

She had been unaware of her grandfather quietly contemplating her mutinous face, his long fingers idly tracing the engraving on a silver-topped cane as he correctly interpreted her thoughts, but had looked up in time to catch his smile, a slight thinning of the lips that betrayed the cruel mockery she had always sensed within him. Nonno Rossi could be lavishly generous, indulgent to a fault, yet he could also be unkind—why else, when he knew how much she longed to live with him permanently, was the subject never broached? He enjoyed her company, of that she was certain, also he enjoyed tremendously parading his beautiful granddaughter before the eyes of envious friends, but most of all, she suspected, he enjoyed wielding power and de-rived perverse satisfaction from keeping her dangling like grapes upon the vine until he felt the moment was right for plucking.

'Do you see much of your cousin Rosalba when you are in England?'

The softly-spoken question had surprised her. So far as she could recall, it was the first time he had spoken his other granddaughter's name.

'I visit her occasionally.' Her voice had betrayed surprise. 'I would never meet up with her otherwise as she never goes out, seemingly being quite happy to return home each night to keep her mother company. But then they never did socialise much, not even when Uncle Angelo was alive.'

She had noted the quiver of pain that had crossed his proud features at the mention of his son. As if he blamed her for this show of weakness, his voice had been chilly in the extreme when he had instructed —no, *demanded*: 'I should like your cousin Rosalba to come with you on your next visit. If you can bring this about, you shall not go unrewarded.'

At the prospect of new clothes, furs and jewellery disappearing before her eyes, Aprile returned to pleading with her cousin.

'Rosalba, you owe it to Grandfather to pay him a visit—you are, after all, the only child of his eldest son, the only descendant who bears his name, yet he's never yet set eyes upon you. He's becoming very frail,' she murmured the lie, 'and his dearest wish is that he might see you before he dies. How can you possibly refuse him . . .?'

As Aprile expected, her cousin's blue eyes clouded with distress. So tender-hearted she found it hard to combat even such blatant emotional blackmail, she choked out:

'I'd hate to upset Grandfather Rossi, but you know the circumstances as well as I do, Aprile, so there's no need for me to elaborate on why a visit to my grandfather is impossible. It's a question,' she concluded gently, 'of loyalty to my mother and also to my father's memory.'

Aprile's lips tightened, yet she fought to keep her tone light as she waved the argument aside. 'Pooh! Water under the bridge!'

Rosalba's reaction was a pitying smile. 'Such an attitude is totally alien to the Sicilian temperament, and well you know it,' she reprimanded.

'But you're half English and your mother is wholly English, so that excuse doesn't apply,' Aprile countered triumphantly. 'Often, in years past, when your mother intervened in our childish spats, she lectured us both thoroughly on the virtue of forgiveness and the need to appreciate an opposing point of view. Don't shatter my illusions by implying that your mother doesn't follow her own teaching!'

She knew better than to expect to draw sparks from the cousin whose serenity she found aggravating, so was not surprised by Rosalba's quiet reply.

'Mother has never spoken to me of our Sicilian relatives. I know only that a great rift developed between my father and Grandfather Rossi and that as a consequence my parents suffered much hurt. However, the details of the matter were never discussed in my hearing so I can't begin to apportion blame. This much, though, I do know,' when Rosalba's chin tilted Aprile glimpsed in her cousin for the very first time a hint of Rossi pride, 'should my mother ever decide to acquaint me with the facts I shall know for certain that every word she says is true, because I've never known her to be anything other than utterly honest and scrupulously fair. Have you?'

Aprile squirmed, knowing the assessment to be true, feeling ashamed of trying to cast doubt, however slight, upon a woman whose gentle kindness had impressed itself so indelibly upon her childish mind that she had at one time been convinced that she was a saint and as a consequence had spent many futile hours peering at the space above her aunt's head, hoping for a glimpse of the halo which would prove her surmise correct.

Her own volatile, Italian mother had been partly to blame for the misconception. Whenever trouble had befallen the family it was to her sister-in-law she had run, and never in vain. Living in a strange country and struggling to learn a new language had not helped to keep difficulties to a minimum, but however often she had been called upon Rosalba's mother had reacted with unfailing kindness, putting aside her own problems, her own considerable chores, until her sister-in-law's fears had been allayed. Aprile's mother's gratitude had always taken the same vocal form. '*Grazie, grazie,* dearest Anna, I swear you are a saint sent from heaven to lighten my burden!'

Once, after tiring of her fruitless search, Aprile had pointed to one of the holy pictures crammed upon the walls of their house and questioned innocently: 'Did those blessed saints keep their haloes in their pockets when they weren't wearing them, Mamma?'

'Heavens!' Her mother had thrown her hands in the air. 'The questions you ask, child! A halo is not something that can be played with like a hoop, it is a nimbus of light which is never visible to the living. To be recognised as a saint one must be canonised, and that is something that can take place only after death.'

'You mean I must wait until Aunt Anna is dead before I see her halo?' Aprile had wailed. Her fantasy had been shattered seconds later by her mother's laughter. And yet, to this very day, a little of it still lingered. . . .

She dragged her thoughts back into the present. Though Rosalba had inherited her mother's sunny disposition she also possessed a little of the same stubbornness and pride that had prevented the rift between members of the Rossi family from healing. If she were to gain the rich rewards her grandfather had dangled before her like a carrot before a donkey, she would need to stretch her persuasive tongue to its uttermost. Abandoning coercion in favour of wistful appeal, she fixed Rosalba with a soulful gaze and sighed:

'For my own sake, I wish you would reconsider. The journey south by train is lonely and tedious, sometimes even frightening, because to a certain type of man a girl travelling alone is considered easy prey. Each year it seems to get worse, until now I find the prospect so nerve-racking I have to steel myself to go.'

She suppressed a smile of satisfaction when her

cousin gasped a protest. 'Then why go?'

Bringing into play every ounce of acting ability she possessed, Aprile replied sadly: 'If ever you'd experienced the joy of Grandfather's greeting, seen the pride with which he introduces me to his friends as: "My granddaughter Aprile, who each year undertakes the long journey from England and forfeits her few precious holiday weeks simply to ease an old man's loneliness", if you could see the sorrow in his eyes when I leave him, hear the hope in his voice when he urges from me the promise that next year I'll return, then believe me, Rosalba, you would have no need to ask me that question.'

Her optimism rose at the sight of Rosalba's troubled frown. She bided her time, allowing silence to reign while she studied the expressions flitting across her cousin's expressive face, reading signs of reluctance, indecision, dismay, then finally resignation. Rosalba was a typical English beauty, she thought, glancing slyly from under lowered lids to assess small feet neatly crossed; small hands twisting nervously in her lap; a wand-slim body; creamy skin, and a soft, vulnerable mouth that collapsed into trembles whenever she was upset. Liquid blue eyes framed by thick dark lashes seemed to dominate a face shaped into an almost perfect oval, and winged eyebrows contrasted dark as charcoal against strands of silver hair tumbling across a brow furrowed with distress.

Yet, unknown to herself, Rosalba had absorbed completely the Sicilian code of family loyalty— every child to be made the object of unrestrained affection; every parent to be venerated almost to the point of idolatry; sisters, cousins—even those far removed—to be included in a violently partisan relationship that no outsider could breach.

It was this strong family tie, combined with concern for her cousin's welfare, that prodded Rosalba into reluctant speech. 'I can't promise anything, Aprile, but I *will* speak to Mother about my accompanying you to Sicily. When she learns of the dangers you face on the journey she'll be as appalled as I am.'

Aprile twirled with delight and clapped her hands. '*Bene, bene! Grazie*, Rosalba. If you can persuade your mother to allow you to come with me you won't regret it—indeed, you'll enjoy it so much you'll probably spend the rest of your life being grateful to me!'

On this score Rosalba had grave doubts. She had no desire to journey abroad, no wish to meet the grandfather whose presence had always loomed in the background of her life but about whom she was not the least bit curious. Just the mention of his name was enough to cause her mother's usually happy features to cloud over with sadness, and never once, so far as she could recollect, had her father so much as acknowledged the existence of his elderly parent. Indeed, it had been easy to forget that her father was not completely English, so keenly had he practised the manners and customs of his adopted country. English was the only language spoken in their house, only English dishes were served at their table, and in place of the traditional Sicilian offering of wine, guests were given the choice of tea or coffee or, should the occasion demand it, whisky or beer.

She waited until her favourite time of day before broaching the subject of her visit to Sicily. After a simple dinner she and her mother cleared the table, carried the dishes into the kitchen to be washed later, then took a tray containing coffee pot and cups into their small sitting-room. From force of habit Rosalba reached out to switch off the main light leaving the room bathed in the subdued glow of table lamps that cast an orange glow over comfortable chairs and dark polished wood furniture, creating the atmosphere her father had sought each evening to establish, a warm, cosy cocoon within which his beloved wife and daughter were protected from the harsh realities of the outside world.

She waited until she sensed that her mother was completely relaxed before venturing: 'Would it distress you, Mother, if I should suggest going with Aprile on her next visit to Sicily?'

Her mother paused in the act of lifting her cup to her lips, changed her mind, and laid it carefully into its saucer. 'Distressed is hardly the word I would choose to describe my reaction to such an idea—worried is perhaps a better definition.'

Puzzled by an air of tension, Rosalba frowned. 'I'm worried too. Aprile has confided that she finds the train journey to the airport frightening—seemingly she's been accosted by unsavoury characters on more than one occasion.'

Her mother's lips seemed stiff as she tried to smile. 'And you want to act as her protector?'

Rosalba flushed, sensing dry mockery. 'As a

mouse would protect a lion?' she quipped wryly. 'No, Mother, I'm well aware of my shortcomings in that respect. But you must admit that there would be less likelihood of Aprile being approached if she had a travelling companion.'

Wondering at the extent of her daughter's naïveté, Mrs Rossi carefully placed her cup and saucer on the tray and tried not to sound incredulous. 'Aprile has actually put forward fear of travelling alone as an excuse to get you to accompany her?' Bewildered by the unaccustomed note of cynicism in her mother's voice, Rosalba nodded, then was further astonished when her mother continued hardly: 'That I do not believe! That young woman is more than capable of looking after herself, she must have some ulterior motive. In fact, it's my guess that it's your Grandfather Rossi who's the instigator behind the request.'

She turned aside, but was not quick enough to hide the glint of tears that had spurted to her eyes.

Appalled, Rosalba slid to her knees to bury her face in her mother's lap. 'I'm so sorry,' she mumbled, 'I had no intention of hurting you. Forget Grandfather Rossi, forget everything I've said—I wouldn't dream of going to Sicily if the thought of it causes you pain.'

'Shush, child . . .' She felt her mother's hand upon her head and relaxed, relieved to hear a voice that was once again calm. 'It was not the thought of your going to Sicily that upset me, but the memories it revived of your father. It's almost two years since he died,' she trembled, 'yet his loss is no more bearable.'

'He wouldn't have wanted me to visit Grandfather?' Rosalba questioned in a murmur.

'No, my dear, he would not,' her mother replied with certainty, 'and I think it's time you were made aware of the reason why.'

Rosalba settled more comfortably against her mother's knee, sensing that what she was about to hear was not so much an explanation as the shedding of a burden.

'In order for you to begin to understand your father's attitude, it's necessary for me to outline first of all a little of your grandfather's character. Whatever I may tell you is, of course, hearsay, but knowing how just and truthful a man your father was I have no compunction about repeating his words.' Huskily, as if relating a story that had no basis in modern life, she continued: 'The family Rossi is, and for centuries past has been, a very rich, very influential family, which may help to explain, if not to excuse, the fact that your grandfather Rossi was considered by his family to be a domineering tyrant whose commands were never to be questioned, whose every desire had to be fulfilled the moment he made it known. As children, your father and your Aunt Caterina grew up accepting that his word was law and never dared question his authority. With everyone, his wife, his servants, his workers, he was strict, but with his children he was extremely so, insisting that they work long hours in the vineyards sharing the work of the labourers. He also vetted their friends, but as he allowed them so little time for recreation it hardly mattered that few of them met with his approval, because they saw so little of them.'

Rosalba stiffened with indignation, but did not try to interrupt when her mother continued, concentrating hard as if having difficulty in recalling details that had been related only once many years previously.

'Sicilians do not pay their children for their labours. All profits from business or estates are put into a family pool and all expenses are met from this pool—pocket money, clothing, even the ring a man places upon the finger of his betrothed is paid for out of the family pool, consequently a son, however hard he has worked, is kept virtually penniless.'

'But what happens when he wants to marry and set up a home of his own?' Curiosity drove Rosalba to interrupt.

'Depending upon the size of his parents' house, he is given either a suite of rooms for himself and his bride or, if the house is too small, an extra floor is added. Sons, you see, are expected to remain always with their family, whereas a daughter when she marries takes her husband's family as her own.'

'How feudal!' Rosalba wondered aloud, her eyes incredulous.

'The Sicilians have always been a feudal race, my dear. The war swept away a lot of the old attitudes, so far as the populations of the larger towns and cities were concerned, but in the isolated country areas and especially in the mountain villages life goes on exactly as it did centuries ago. The war was responsible for the upheaval in your father's life. Not even Conte Rossi's influence could prevent his son from being drafted into the army. He was twenty years of age when he left home, and was told only the night before he was due to leave that his father had just concluded arrangements for his marriage to a girl whose face he couldn't even recall. However, as he had so little time left, he decided not to argue but to sort out the matter when he returned on his first leave.'

Rosalba shot upright. 'His father arranged for him to marry a girl he hardly knew!'

'Such was the manner of the man,' her mother nodded.

'But what about my grandmother, couldn't she have intervened?'

'Your father mentioned her only once,' her mother frowned, 'when he expressed a wish that you should be named after her, but I seem to recall your Aunt Caterina mentioning that she died when she and your father were in their teens.'

'Do go on, Mother! I'm dying to know how Father managed to escape.'

For the first time since their talk had begun her mother laughed aloud. 'He *escaped*, as you put it, by being taken prisoner, before he was due to take his first leave. He was sent here to England and interned in a camp just a few miles from where I lived.'

'He was imprisoned!'

'No, dear,' her mother chuckled. 'Italian prisoners of war were dealt with very leniently by the authorities. Each day they were allowed out of the camp to work on nearby farms; I was a land girl working on the farm to which your father was sent.'

Rosalba's nose wrinkled. 'How unromantic!'

'How wrong you are!' Her mother smiled, her

eyes dreamy. 'However,' she continued briskly, 'on that subject I don't intend to elaborate, except to say that we fell in love and were married immediately the war ended. Now, Rosalba, do you think you could make a fresh pot of coffee? My throat is parched with all this talking.'

'What, *now* ...?' Rosalba protested. 'But I want to hear how Grandfather reacted—and what about the girl Father was supposed to marry, did she——'

'Later!' her mother insisted firmly. 'I refuse to continue until you've given me some more coffee.'

'*Really*, Mother!' Rosalba jumped to her feet and stood poised, ready to run into the kitchen. 'At times you can be so *aggravating!*'

Her mother relaxed when Rosalba left the room. Raking over dead ashes had taken more out of her than she was prepared to admit. The coffee had been an excuse; she needed a pause in which to re-armour a heart bared by memories of a man with whom she had shared a love that had been as strong on the day that he died as it had been on the day of their marriage. All she wanted in life was to see Rosalba achieve the same happiness, which was why she had reacted so violently against the idea of her visiting Città del Monte, the village perched high upon a mountain in the shadow of the castle that had been her husband's former home—the 'Castle of the Fountains' within whose walls he had experienced nothing but unhappiness. She shuddered, feeling a chill of foreboding as she remembered one dreary, unforgettable day when, shortly after taking the plunge into business, from the hour of opening until

closing time they had had to cope with one catastrophe after another.

'How long will it be before you regret marrying
me, Angelo?' she had whispered, finally bending
beneath the strain. 'How long before you're wishing
yourself back home in your castle on a mountain
top?'

'It was never my home,' he had replied simply,
pulling her into his arms. 'The Castle of the Fountains was my father's stage, I was merely expected to
play the occasional bit part if ever the script called
for it. My home is here, where *I* am the star and you
and Rosalba are my adoring audience!'

She was quite composed by the time Rosalba returned with a fresh pot of coffee. After hastily pouring her mother a cup, Rosalba resumed her former
position on the floor, her feet tucked beneath her,
her shoulder supported by her mother's knee.

'Now carry on, Mother, before I die of suspense!'

Deliberately her mother sugared her coffee and
tasted it before continuing. 'There's not much more
to add. Your father wrote to your grandfather telling him of our marriage and of his decision to remain in England. Predictably, your grandfather was
furious, so furious that he sent your Aunt Caterina
and her husband to try to persuade him to return
home. The fact that they, too, decided they preferred poverty-stricken freedom to wealthy tyranny
and elected to stay in England did nothing to
sweeten his temper. He disowned them both, refused even to allow them to have the few small personal pieces they'd left at the castle. However, we
managed,' she continued lightly. 'We worked until

we'd amassed enough capital to invest in the bakery business which we had both decided would suit us. It was hard, back-breaking work, and for the first few years we made no profit at all, just enough to cover the overheads. Then your father began experimenting with continental confectionery and fancy breads, and from then onwards we found it difficult to keep up with demand. We didn't make a fortune —just a comfortable living—but that was all we ever wanted. And not until we'd been married ten years could we afford to consider a family.'

She drew in a steadying breath and by deliberately avoiding mentioning her husband managed to continue. 'A couple of years ago your Aunt Caterina was surprised to receive a letter from your grandfather asking for news of any grandchildren which he might possess and begging that they might be allowed to visit him. The invitation was not extended to his own children. Your aunt was most upset—the letter was couched in such self-pitying terms she couldn't avoid being so—and possessing, as she does, a strong sense of duty she existed for months in a state of mournful weeping, lighting candle after candle while she prayed to be excused her neglect of her aged father.

'Strangely, your own father remained completely unmoved and refused to allow you to visit your grandfather, not because of any feeling of spite, but because he was mistrustful of his father's motives.' She relaxed with a sigh, supporting her head against the back of her chair. 'And there the matter has rested—until now.'

Rosalba sat back on her heels and spelled out

slowly: 'I think Grandfather Rossi must be utterly despicable! I shall tell Aprile tomorrow that she must travel alone, because I have less wish than ever to visit him.'

'Perhaps it would be wise, dear,' her mother murmured, her eyes half-closed, 'he's sure to start matchmaking. Much better to stay at home and marry some nice young Englishman.' She opened her eyes, prepared to smile, but her lips stiffened at the hint of frozen fear she glimpsed in her daughter's eyes before dark lashes swept down on to fiery cheeks.

Hastily, Rosalba jumped to her feet. 'I shall never marry, Mother, my mind is quite made up.'

Her mother stared at her retreating back, rendered dumb with astonishment and dismay. There had been no hint of coyness in Rosalba's voice, no girlish invitation to be contradicted; her statement had been one of sheer panic-stricken revulsion.

Her mother slumped back in her chair. 'Angelo, how blindly selfish we've been!' she gasped, realising just at that moment how much their protective cosseting was responsible for their daughter's shy immaturity. 'Help me,' she breathed a silent prayer to the husband whose wise counsel she sorely missed, 'show me how to crack the shell so that the bird can fly!'

CHAPTER TWO

ROSALBA's mother waited until breakfast was over the next morning before confounding her daughter with the observation:

'I've been thinking, dear ... perhaps I was too hasty in condemning your trip to Sicily.' Rosalba shot her a look of astonishment, but as her lips began framing an argument her mother frowned. 'Now hear me out! I've given the subject a lot of thought—in fact, all night I've wrestled with my conscience, trying to decide what your father's ultimate reaction would have been had his attitude been given time to mellow. Perhaps I should have encouraged him to make peace with his father, because I now realise that had he had no affection whatsoever for him he wouldn't have found it so difficult to forgive. He was proud, yet the ties of kinship are very strong—more so between Sicilians than those of any other race—which is why I feel certain that, given sufficient time, your father and grandfather would eventually have become reconciled.'

Rosalba was utterly confused by her mother's abrupt *volte-face*. She stared at her, attempted to speak, then changed her mind. Finally, however, she had to respond to her mother's silent anxiety. 'I ... I can't help feeling you're mistaken,' she contradicted, blue eyes dark with puzzlement. 'Aren't you forgetting that Sicily is the land of the vendetta where quarrels are never allowed to die out and grudges are forever refuelled and handed down from generation to generation like some macabre inheritance?'

'It's also the land of the blood pact,' her mother reminded her, 'where men who are unrelated slash their wrists in order to mingle their blood and swear fidelity. Once such a pact has been made they consider themselves blood brothers. So how can you think that a quarrel between father and son would be left unresolved when both belong to a land where an ounce of blood is considered to be worth more than a pound of friendship?'

Rosalba pushed a heavy wing of hair back from her brow, looking utterly confounded. 'You could be right, I suppose. Personally, I don't think I shall ever understand the race; from what little I've heard, they impress me as being completely uncivilised.' When her mother laughed aloud, Rosalba insisted: 'Well, how else should I think when I hear talk of tyrannical grandfathers; men who inflict wounds upon themselves in order to establish friendship; vendettas that last for centuries and even, according to Aprile, bandits who roam the hills and attack innocent people even in this day and age. No, Mother, the more I hear of Sicily the less inclined I am to visit it. Let's just forget the whole idea, shall we?' she urged, feeling a sudden unaccountable surge of fear. 'I'm quite happy as I am; why must my life be disrupted for the sake of an autocratic old man?'

But though she argued and pleaded for days afterwards she discovered her mother to be uncharacteristically adamant. Right up until the evening of her departure, as she waited with luggage packed, her handbag containing rail and plane tickets, passport and lire, clutched tightly in her fist, for the arrival of Aprile she tried to coax her mother to change her mind.

'You'll never manage on your own, Mother—as things are you get tired coping with the bakery, so how will you feel having to manage the shop as well?'

'Your Aunt Caterina has promised to help out, as you very well know,' her mother replied, wearied by constant argument, her mind worn out with the worry of whether or not she was doing the right thing. However, it was now too late to back out. Conte Rossi had been informed that both his grand-daughters would be arriving at Palermo airport within the next twenty-four hours—his response had been unreservedly jubilant.

Once she had been on the verge of calling off the trip, and that had been the fault of her sister-in-law, Caterina, who, having heard all the details from Aprile, had rushed to her house in a state of great agitation.

'Anne!' she had gasped. 'Aprile has just told me that Rosalba is to accompany her to Città del Monte —is that true?' In response to a nod of confirmation she had thrown up her hands in horror and babbled like a woman possessed. 'No, no, you must not allow the *innocente* to go, it is too *pericoloso* ... too ... *dangerous*!'

Though the blood had cooled to ice in her veins Anne Rossi had laughed and tried to sound unconcerned. 'What nonsense you talk, Caterina! They are two young girls setting off to spend a short holi-day with their grandfather—what possible danger could befall them?'

Caterina had rushed forward to grab her arm, shaking her fiercely as words tumbled from her lips. 'Have you forgotten that my brother Angelo was be-trothed to a girl from Città del Monte and that when he did not return, and married you instead, that girl would be considered sullied, an object of pity? Do you imagine that he remained an exile from choice? If you did, then I can assure you, Anne, that you were wrong. Angelo did not return to visit his father because he knew his life would be forfeit the moment he stepped upon Sicilian soil.'

Within the sane atmosphere of an English sitting-room the theory Caterina had propounded had sounded like the plot of a comic opera, and Anne had told her sister-in-law this in no uncertain terms, ending with the derisive question: 'And even if such a ridiculous situation were to exist, what possible connection could it have with Rosalba?'

In a mighty huff, Caterina had shrugged away, muttering darkly. 'Rosalba must inherit her father's debts. It is from her that the *famiglia* Diavolo will expect to collect its dues. I realise, Anne, that you look upon me as a superstitious fool, but believe me, every word I speak is the truth. What puzzles me greatly,' she had croaked, 'is that my father must know it too.'

When the doorbell chimed, announcing Aprile's arrival, Rosalba resigned herself to the inevitable and turned to give her mother a last farewell hug.

'Goodbye, dear, look after yourself, don't work too hard!'

Wrestling with an avalanche of last-minute doubts, it was as much as her mother could do to return the hug and murmur huskily: 'Enjoy yourself, sweetheart. I know you're reluctant to go, but two weeks will soon pass.'

When the taxi departed, taking the two girls on the first stage of their journey, Anne Rossi returned slowly to the house, collapsed into a chair and gave way to tears. 'Look after her, Angelo,' she choked. 'Wherever you are, my darling, please try to protect our child. Try to understand that it's for her own sake that I've sent her away. We smothered her in security, you and I, she must have her chance to breathe, to sweat, to roll up her sleeves and plunge both hands into life up to the elbows. She must learn how to love—or even just to think she has loved!'

The train was due to depart for London at midnight. Rosalba viewed the five-hour journey with trepidation, yet prepared to protect her cousin as a tigress would protect her cub. Aprile's dark, Latin beauty attracted attention wherever she went; even as she swayed down the corridor of the train in Rosalba's wake, strange eyes lingered to enjoy the sight of a proud head capped with hair black as a raven's wing, flirtatious eyes, and a voluptuous figure shown off to perfection by the latest style of Italian knitwear, a clinging, cobweb-fine two-piece, its colour exactly matching the poppy red, half-smiling, half-pouting mouth.

As Rosalba dumped their hand luggage on to a seat in an empty compartment, two young men who had been dozing in the adjoining compartment jumped to their feet, now wide awake, and slid back the door.

'Please join us in here!' one of them begged politely.

Mistrusting the way his eyes were roving Aprile's curves, Rosalba stuttered.

'Certainly not, we prefer to be alone, if you don't mind.' She waited for Aprile to follow her and was amazed when her cousin hesitated, then drawled:

'Don't be stuffy, Rosalba! There's no better way to shorten a dreary train journey than with lively conversation. As these two gentlemen are prepared to entertain us, it would be churlish of us to refuse their invitation.'

Rosalba's scandalised gasp was ignored as eager hands transferred their luggage from one compartment to the other. When they were both seated opposite the two men, Aprile relaxed and began chatting, quite at ease, but Rosalba remained silent, stiffly erect. Even when they proved to be pleasant, harmless companions she could not unbend. In no time at all Aprile had elicited the information that they were student doctors returning from a holiday in Scotland. Both vied with each other to keep Aprile amused, relating funny incidents that had occurred on hospital wards which, though they kept Aprile in stitches, Rosalba could not help thinking would have appalled their innocent patients.

For the life of her she could not respond, but drew deeper and deeper into her silent shell until, by the time the train had drawn into Euston station, her companions had almost forgotten her existence. She did manage to gasp her appreciation of their insistence on carrying their luggage to the taxi which was to take them to Victoria where they would then catch a connecting train to Gatwick airport. It was still early morning as they said their goodbyes, the two men openly envious that their holiday was now ended and the girls' just about to begin.

'What about us meeting up again a fortnight from now?' Aprile's most besotted admirer pleaded. 'If you break your journey and stay a few extra hours in London we could show you the sights.' Refusing to be thwarted, he scribbled a telephone number on a scrap of paper and thrust it into Aprile's hand.

Rosalba felt moved to protest. 'Aprile, you know we can't! These two gentlemen have both been very kind, but after all, we hardly know them.'

In the early morning air of a cosmopolitan city just stirring into life where, just across the street, a cinema hoarding was advertising in lurid detail a torrid sex film; where a nearby news stand was displaying girlie magazines with front covers that left nothing to the imagination; where girls high-stepped past wearing tee-shirts emblazoned with suggestive invitations and young men showed pride in their masculinity with the help of skin-tight jeans, her words sounded like an echo from a generation long past. To her acute embarrassment, Aprile and one of the young doctors collapsed into laughter. But the other championed her by rebuking quietly:

'Don't knock modesty, it makes a refreshing change from being assaulted on all sides by bra-less females flaunting their liberation by inviting every man in their vicinity to jump into bed with them.'

Rosalba had had enough. Ducking inside the taxi, she huddled in a corner, despising herself for the blush that was scorching her cheeks, hating her own cowardice, wishing with all her heart that she could master the art of sophisticated, brittle conversation, being made more and more conscious the farther she travelled from home of her miserable social inadequacies.

Showing a supreme confidence Rosalba envied, Aprile paid off the taxi when they eventually reached Victoria, instructed a porter to take charge of their luggage, then began ushering her cousin through the huge labyrinth, barely needing to glance at a bewildering array of arrows positioned to direct travellers to various platforms. Hating the noise, the bustle, the cold impersonality of her surroundings, Rosalba wished fervently that she had remained at home.

Aprile's attitude puzzled her. From the moment their journey had begun she had demonstrated plainly how irked she was by her cousin's naïveté and how little she was in need of a protective companion. Rosalba suspected that for some obscure reason she had been tricked into coming, but for the life of her she could not understand why.

Following blindly in her cousin's wake, she was unaware of the obstacle in her path until she felt the ground moving under her feet. With a cry of alarm she jumped back, narrowly avoiding collision with one of the queue of people streaming towards the moving staircase. Panic-stricken, she watched Aprile being borne downward and out of sight, but not even the threat of being left stranded could compel her to set foot on what to her eyes was a terrifying contraption. Tense with fear, knuckles showing white as she gripped hard upon her handbag, she stared at the back of Aprile's head as she retreated into the distance, willing her to look around.

At the crucial moment she did so, and even from a distance Rosalba could recognise angry incredulity in the dark eyes that searched, then eventually discovered her.

Rosalba remained where she was, trembling, trying to decide which of two evils was preferable, the dangerous-looking staircase or Aprile's equally dangerous temper. Just as she had decided that nothing on earth would persuade her to set foot on the moving steps of the lethal ladder that plunged so steeply she felt sick just peering down the length of it, Aprile reappeared, her face reflecting scornful disgust. If she had not already begun to guess that her cousin considered her an unwelcome burden, Aprile's angry reaction would have clarified the situation immediately.

'Must you shame me by standing there dithering like a country bumpkin? Come along!' Before Rosalba realised her intention Aprile gripped her by the elbow and jerked hard, impelling her forward so that she stumbled on to a vacant stair. Wildly she grabbed for the handrail, her stomach heaving against the rapid descent, her eyes so tightly closed she would probably have fallen when she reached the bottom had Aprile not pushed her off just in time.

One glance at her ashen face was enough to cause Aprile to relent.

'Sit down for a minute.' She pushed Rosalba on to a nearby bench. 'You look ready to collapse.' She waited without speaking until Rosalba's spasms of trembling had ceased, then realising that she had been genuinely terrified, she sighed her exasperation. 'What an incredibly timid mouse you are! I'm sorry I was so rough, but in fairness to myself I must point out that the majority of people would find such a display of jitters unbelievable. The escalator is a perfectly safe method of transporting people from one level to another. Look,' she urged, 'see how casually it's accepted by everyone else!'

Taking a grip upon her nerves, Rosalba glanced sideways just as a girl of about eight years of age began skipping from one stair to another, her enthusiasm having to be curbed by a rebuke from her mother. Then with cheeks hot, she glanced shamefacedly at Aprile. 'I'm sorry,' she gulped, 'you must despise me very much.'

Humour restored, Aprile hauled her to her feet. 'It's not your fault,' she reassured her cheerfully, 'your parents are most to blame for incarcerating you in a convent school then insisting upon you working with them in the shop instead of chucking you out into the world where you would have mixed with youngsters of your own age. Your father may have been dedicated to the English way of life, but in his attitude towards his daughter he remained completely Sicilian. There's no doubt about it,

Rosalba,' she sighed, 'you're definitely a one-off, a complete enigma to your own generation. I'll do whatever I can to help repair the damage, but you'll have to co-operate. We have only a fortnight, so be a devil,' she jeered kindly, 'and determine to make the most of it!'

Rosalba's first impulse was to defend her parents, but, as was her way when troubled, she retreated into her shell to sort out her thoughts and to digest all that Aprile had said.

Silence was so much a part of Rosalba's nature that Aprile now took it for granted. Some years earlier, after one of their family gatherings, she had protested to her mother: 'It's not natural, the way Rosalba tucks herself into a corner and sits for hours without saying a word! Whenever she's spoken to she replies only in monosyllables, so it's hardly surprising that she's ignored—one tends to forget she's there!'

'If only one were able to do the same with you,' her mother had scolded dryly. Then realising that her daughter was genuinely concerned, she had consoled: 'You my dear, are of a nature that finds it hard to accept that not everyone wants to be the centre of attraction. Rosalba is a solitary soul but a happy one. She speaks if she has something to say, but otherwise remains silent, a silence born not of moods but of a serenity of the spirit found only in those endowed with a truly happy nature. If you take the trouble to study your cousin you'll discover that she takes a bright-eyed interest in all that's being said, and though her words are sparing she is

more than generous with her sweet smiles. Believe
me, little worrier, Rosalba is more to be envied than
pitied, for she was born with a tranquillity many
people would spend a fortune to possess.'

Since then, Aprile had never found her cousin's
silences uncomfortable, which was why she made no
attempt to chat and spoke only a few reassuring
words when, sitting side by side in the plane with
seat belts fastened awaiting take-off, she sensed
Rosalba's apprehension as the scream of jet engines
assaulted their ears.

'Are you all right?' she yelled above the noise.

Petrified, but trying not to show it, Rosalba nodded. Determination triumphed over a strong inclination to be sick as the plane rumbled across the
tarmac, then, with nauseating suddenness, became
airborne.

She refused all the refreshments that were offered,
averting her eyes from the sight of Aprile who, after
she had demolished her own breakfast, began making inroads into the one Rosalba had spurned. Once
she dared a look out of the window and though, in
different circumstances, the sight of sun shining
upon rugged mountains with mist-scarves wreathed
around their peaks would have delighted her, she
quickly looked away.

'Aprile is right!' she began a secret scolding, unaware that her fingernails were gouging her palms.
'You're a martyr to the most mortifying infirmity
know to man—or woman! Cowardice! If you're
to avoid living the rest of your life in imagined
agony you must find the courage to tackle each bull

encountered by the horns instead of running for shelter behind a five-barred gate!'

'Ladies and gentlemen,' the pilot addressed his passengers over the intercom, 'we are now approaching our destination. If you look below you'll see Palermo.'

Without thinking, Rosalba followed his instruction and gasped. The sun was shining down upon a city trapped within a shell of mountains. The air seemed to glitter, adding extra sparkle to the breathtaking landscape, emphasising the violet and purple of the hills, the vivid green of the plains, the white and russet tones of the towers, domes and steeples clustered within the ancient city. Beyond shone the deep blue sea and far in the distance white foam broke over jagged rocks.

Palermo! City enclosed within a *baccello d'oro.* Was she to become a willing or an unwilling prisoner inside the golden shell?

CHAPTER THREE

FIVE minutes after stepping out of the plane they both became aware of an oppressive heat being generated by the light woollen suits they had found so essential in England. Sweat began trickling between Rosalba's shoulder-blades as she queued with the rest of the passengers at passport control.

Jauntily, Aprile stepped up to the desk, had her passport scrutinised and returned by a uniformed official whose dour expression was enough to make Rosalba quake at the knees. Nervousness caused her hand to tremble when her turn came and perhaps—she consoled herself—that was why the official took his time with her passport, noting intently all the relevant details. Her pulses began hammering when, without a word of explanation, he beckoned to someone standing out of sight behind her.

Seemingly quite impervious to the impatient fidgeting of the remainder of the queue, a man strode forward and extended one brown, slim-fingered hand for her passport. She became conscious that her heart was pounding rapidly, her palms sweating, her eyes wide with apprehension as she waited for the stranger to conclude his examination. She told herself that she had nothing to fear, yet within his tall shadow she felt intimidated.

He was not an official, she decided, otherwise he would be wearing uniform, but in spite of his casual attire of a cotton, safari-type shirt mere shades lighter than his tan and matching cotton slacks, he exuded an air of authority. Perhaps it was the arrogant tilt of a head covered with black short-cropped hair that looked as if, given the slightest leeway, it would curl up tightly as the fleece of a ram. Or again, it might have been eyes set above a high-bridged nose that arrowed downward to flaring nostrils, eyes of forbidding darkness that had bestowed upon her a glance so sharp it had sliced off her breath.

When finally he handed back her passport, his cool politeness was something of an anti-climax.

'Thank you. I hope you enjoy your stay on our island, Signorina *Rossi*.'

Rosalba's highly intuitive senses reared against the manner in which he had spoken her name, rolling it around his tongue as if savouring its taste. In such an anticipatory way might a leopard have regarded the fruits of a day's hunting, congratulating himself upon his success yet prepared to wait a while before devouring his prey. She sensed plainly the animosity behind his polite façade and was puzzled by it, so felt unable to raise her eyes higher than the buckle clinching his belt, a buckle so barbaric it alone was sufficient to repel. It was of solid gold, she guessed, deeply engraved to throw into sharp relief the figure of an unidentifiable jungle beast with fangs bared, poised as if to spring upon a huge cobra coiled to strike.

'Thank you, *s-signore*,' she stammered, grabbing her passport. 'And goodbye.'

'*Arrivederci, signorina*,' he stressed softly, dismissing her with a mocking bow.

Aprile, who had been an avid spectator, pounced on her flustered cousin the moment she reached her side. 'Who on earth was he? What did he want? What did he have to say?'

'Nothing much,' Rosalba gulped, brushing a hand across a flushed cheek. 'He just wished me a pleasant stay on the island.'

'He took all that time just to say that?'

'He seemed very interested in my passport.'

'Ah!' Aprile snapped her fingers and looked satisfied. 'So it was not so much the book as its title that attracted his attention. Even in Palermo the name Rossi is a force to be reckoned with! Which reminds me, we must hurry. I expect Grandfather's car is parked outside the airport entrance, and we mustn't keep him waiting.'

They stepped outside into dazzling sunshine and for a second Rosalba found it difficult to focus upon the man Aprile hailed, then ran quickly to embrace. When her vision cleared she saw an elegant man, elderly but upright, rapier-slim, with steel-grey hair, eyes that pierced, and thin lips, sternly chiselled, which when he greeted them relaxed into an indulgent smile. She hung back, repelled yet fascinated by the man who was so like and yet so unlike her own dear father. The height was the same—not tall, yet seeming so because of the upright stance and incredible slenderness that she herself had inherited. The same brown eyes, yet where her father's eyes had reflected tenderness the Conte's seemed to possess a pebble-hard core. It was when, still hugging Aprile, he stared across her shoulder and sent a smile in her own direction, that she decided that whatever faint resemblance he might have to her father ceased immediately it reached his mouth—a mouth that widened without warmth as if responding mechanically to a command to smile.

'So this is Rosalba...!' Releasing Aprile, who immediately dived into the interior of a sleek grey limousine, he strode forward. 'Welcome to Sicily, *nipotina*,' then when she remained immobile, he encouraged gently, 'Well, *viso d'angelo*, aren't you going to greet your *nonno* with a kiss?'

Reluctantly she stepped towards him, suppressing a shiver of revulsion, wondering why, as he bent his head to place a light kiss upon her lips, she should suddenly be reminded of the stranger's barbaric buckle that had borne the symbol of a coiled snake.

As she sank into a seat upholstered in soft grey suede she thought how well the rich, warm, almost sensuous setting suited her suave grandfather who, seeming to sense the exhaustion that had descended upon her like a cloud, did not attempt to engage her in conversation but relaxed in his seat, seemingly content to watch different expressions chasing across her features when, with a fat kiss of tyres against tarmac, the car glided away from the airport and headed in the direction of the ancient city of Palermo.

'Rather than subject you two girls to yet another tiring journey, I have arranged for us to stay the night in the capital. After a refreshing night's sleep, you will be better able to enjoy the journey to Città del Monte,' he informed them, then lapsed into a silence which he did not attempt to break until they entered the narrow streets of a capital possessed of unmistakable mystique, retaining among its architecture remnants of the Greek, Roman, Arab, Norman and Spanish invaders who had left indelible impressions in the shape of palaces, mosques, temples and many smaller cameos of beauty.

Rosalba's main impression was one of noise. In the city centre, buses, horse cabs and cars crammed the narrow streets and as traffic slowed down to a crawl it seemed to her thrashed eardrums that thousands of irate drivers had fingers jammed permanently against their horns. Crowds of pedestrians spilled off inadequate pavements and weaved with contemptuous ease in and out of the traffic, ignoring gesticulating drivers, squealing brakes, and even a bombardment of hotly-worded insults fired out of furiously wound-down windows.

When occasionally the surge of humanity parted she caught glimpses of ancient palaces decorated with stone carvings and wrought iron balconies; shady courtyards; bookshops; antique dealers; jewellers and many boutiques whose windows were offering the very latest samples of Italian fashion.

Eventually the car turned into a small piazza and drew up in front of a four-storied building, each story decorated and embellished with *putti*, garlands and marble scrolls. Between the ground floor windows were statues depicting the four seasons; on the first floor was a niche occupied by a stone effigy of some long-forgotten king, and on either side of the windows stone angels kept guard over the lintels.

'This entire *palazzo* belonged at one time to the Rossi family,' her grandfather explained as he ushered Rosalba and Aprile through the front door, 'but now only the ground floor is mine, the other three stories having been renovated, made into self-contained flats, and sold to their present occupiers.'

Rosalba registered a confused impression of pink and grey mosaic floors, grey marble columns supporting a ceiling liberally painted with gold leaf and many narrow, double doors—ornately carved, with finger plates of exquisitely-painted enamel set above and below handles of chased gold—ranged around the hall.

As the chauffeur carried in their luggage a woman apeared bustling across the hall to meet them. '*La povera bambina!*' she exclaimed, her dark eyes brimming with sympathy.

'This is Rita, my housekeeper,' the Conte introduced her, 'who has been in my service for many years. She will show you to your rooms now, for I know you must both be feeling exhausted. Please do not hesitate to ask her for anything you need which has not already been provided.'

But the combination of unaccustomed heat, excitement, and a long, tiring journey proved to be too much for Rosalba who, once she was shown into her room, had eyes for nothing but the huge bed that seemed to beckon her forward.

'Oh, bliss ...!' She sank on to its surface. 'This supplies all my immediate needs, Rita—I intend sleeping for the next twelve hours, at the very least.' When the door closed behind the smiling housekeeper, she undressed, slipped into a nightdress, then crawled between silken sheets. 'Hm!' she almost purred, her lids weighted with sleep. 'Grandfather obviously believes that the quickest way to a woman's heart is to pander to her comfort. I must be wary and remember ...' she smothered a great yawn, 'to treat luxury as a casual acquaintance; any closer intimacy might result in it becoming my master!'

She slept only half the time she had promised herself. It might have been the unaccustomed luxury of the strange bed, or perhaps excitement had penetrated even her deep, soundless sleep, but nevertheless she awoke at six-thirty that evening feeling refreshed and, for one of her temperament, strangely restless.

The city seemed to beckon to be explored and some deep sense of inherited pride urged her to respond. This was the capital city of the land in which her father's family had its roots; already she felt a strong affinity which, had she dwelt upon it, she might have likened to that of an exile who had finally returned home.

Quickly she showered and shrugged into a cotton sundress of a shade that added deep tones of lilac to her blue eyes. Hoping to find a suitable present for her mother as she toured the shops, she stuffed all the lire she possessed into a white handbag, then, hooking it over her wrist, she made her way to the adjoining bedroom hoping to find Aprile awake and eager to keep her company.

She tiptoed into the bedroom darkened by drawn shutters, but realised immediately she heard her cousin's even breathing that she was still asleep. Feeling a little less enthusiastic, she walked slowly along a passageway that terminated in the main hall which was flooded with sunshine spilling through an open doorway. Irresistibly drawn, she stepped outside to the sounds, smells and sights of a city slowly awakening after its siesta. She knew she ought to have sought out Rita or her grandfather to tell them of her plans, but consoled her conscience with the promise: 'If I walk a little way, keeping the piazza always within sight, I can't possibly get lost.'

The piazza lay just off one of the main arteries of the city, so in less than five minutes she found herself in the middle of the shopping centre. Taking great care to steer a straight course so that she would not find the return journey difficult, she strolled through narrow streets, stopping every now and again to peer into windows choked with merchandise, and amusing herself by trying to guess which of the island's many invaders were responsible for the characteristics displayed by the individual faces in the crowd. One man of taller, sturdier stature than the typical Sicilian could have inherited his looks from Albanian ancestors, she decided, whereas a slight, lean little man might have had relatives whose origins lay in North Africa. Two young sailors seemed definitely to owe their blond good looks to the Normans, and an occasional erectly-held head and sweeping stride could belong only to one possessed of Arabian pride.

Small boys swarmed everywhere, their darting eyes assessing each passer-by, hoping to discover a tourist who might be prevailed upon to offer a small tip for acting as a guide or for carrying a parcel. Rosalba smiled, reflecting upon a statement her father had made some years ago. Mocking this small vice peculiar to his race, he had assured her: 'The carrying of parcels is something to be avoided by the bourgeois, who consider that to do so is to lose caste. Everyone wishes to "*far buona figura*", consequently they will do nothing in public that might be classed, even remotely, as menial.'

As she looked around her, she wondered if this attitude were responsible for the fact that everyone was so formally dressed, men wearing stylish suits, silk shirts, and impeccable ties and the women's dresses immaculate and fitting perfectly.

Suddenly her attention was drawn by a glimpse of feverish activity and unusual sounds issuing from a side street so narrow the entrance had almost escaped her attention. As she hesitated she was caught up within a stream of people all heading down the narrow street, so, curiously, she allowed herself to be drawn towards a flight of steeply-descending stone steps leading into an arena within which every available inch of space was taken up by stalls overflowing with every conceivable type of merchandise. Obviously it was a market place, one where the locals shopped for requirements ranging from food to shoe laces. '*The casbah of Palermo*', her grandfather later contemptuously referred to it, a description which she considered very apt.

Completely enthralled by the seething bustle, colour and movement, she moved into the swarming throng, trying to decipher the yells of fishmongers extolling the delights of exotic fish laid out on wooden counters and slabs of ice. Though most were completely strange to her, she recognised red mullet, octopus, sea urchin whose red flesh was supposedly an aphrodisiac, oysters, prawns and swordfish laid out so that their vicious spikes pointed straight into the air.

Many of the fruits displayed were also unfamiliar. Fancying a bright red apple, Rosalba pointed to a box full and held up one finger.

'*Uno!*' She communicated that she required only one. The stallholder could not have been more obliging had she offered to buy the whole box. Carefully he lifted one from its resting place, offered it to her, then changed his mind and discarded it in favour of another, slightly bigger, slightly more red. She accepted with a smile, then opened her handbag to display a crumpled pile of lire.

'How much?' she queried. Then remembering Aprile's conversation with the taxi driver she recalled the appropriate word. '*Quanto . . .?*' She stumbled over the pronunciation, then thrust forward the bag, inviting him to help himself to the required amount.

Once the pleasant exchange had been concluded she strolled deeper into the crowd, sinking small white teeth into the apple which, to her surprise, did not respond with the crisp crunch she had expected but disintegrated with a squelching sound as her teeth penetrated skin soft and smooth as that of a plum and pulp luscious as peach yet with a taste that was definitely superior. Juice escaped in a sticky stream down her chin, but the crowd around her was so dense she had no hope of being allowed sufficient space to search her handbag for a tissue.

She had by this time progressed into what seemed

to be the very heart of the market place, where butchers' blocks a mere quarter of the size of a normal table stood cheek by jowl, a third of each surface taken up by rusty, unhygienic-looking scales that barely left each butcher enough space to wield his knife through cuts of meat that seemed mostly to be veal.

Spying a deserted alleyway leading off from the market place, she elbowed her way towards it, anxious to remove the sticky mess from her chin. Finally she reached it, and with a gasp of relief leant against the wall and began rummaging in her handbag. Absorbed in her task, she did not notice she had company until a shadow fell across her face. Her head jerked upward, the smile on her lips freezing when she saw a youth of about sixteen dressed in tattered jeans and a dirty checked shirt, his swaggering stance echoing the menace in his small, wicked eyes.

She realised his intention immediately his grubby hand snaked out towards her handbag. Instinctively, she snapped it shut and clenched her fists around the rim, resisting the pressure of his hands, determined not to give way without a struggle. She saw his eyes glitter dangerously as he freed one of his hands, raising it to strike, but she did not give in, not even when the flat of his palm connected smartly with her cheek. She saw stars, yet with bulldog tenacity clung on to the bag that had suddenly achieved the status of a treasured possession. Surprisingly, it did not occur to her to scream, even though there were hundreds of shoppers within earshot. When his hand raised a second time, positioned to inflict a karate chop on her bird-boned wrist, she gritted her teeth and closed her eyes.

But the blow did not land. She heard the harsh rasping of a surprised breath in her assailant's throat, felt a slackness when his grip upon her bag was released, and opened her eyes just in time to see a fist cracking painfully against her assailant's chin. Emitting a howl of pain, he staggered backward holding a hand to his bleeding mouth, then, displaying the agility of a monkey, he regained his balance, spun round, then raced for cover into the crowd.

Rosalba sagged against the wall. Now that her ordeal was over her knees seemed to have turned to jelly and her stomach was churning at such a speed she felt certain she was going to vomit. The very idea jerked her upright and though still ashen pale she managed to sound composed as she addressed her rescuer.

'Oh ...!' Her lips framed a rosy ring of surprise. 'It's you ...' she trailed, with unflattering lack of enthusiasm.

'It is I,' the stranger from the airport agreed, his eyes sternly condemning her stupidity. 'Don't you know better,' he questioned coldly, 'than to wander around such places alone? Villains such as that young man are the pests of Palermo, they appear as silently as rats out of the sewers in search of gullible tourists wandering wide-eyed around the shopping areas carrying, with criminal carelessness, every lira they possess in flimsy handbags or easy-to-filch wallets, and what is more, displaying the same each time they make a purchase. Such people present ir-

resistible temptation to young villains. I would not
attempt to defend petty criminals, yet I find it very
difficult to feel sympathy for idiots such as yourself
who proffer an open handbag, tempting a stallholder to cheat, and who wander alone through a
district too notorious for even local housewives to
venture unaccompanied.'

Though his tone might have been politer,
Rosalba, once the facts had been stated, could see
that his annoyance was justified, so, with a
generosity that Aprile would immediately have
recognised, she accepted the implication that she
only had herself to blame. Yet for the life of her she
could say no more than two short words.

'I'm sorry . . .' she faltered.

Suspiciously, his dark eyes raked her troubled
face before he shocked her by grating a colloquial-
ism that fell oddly from his lips.

'Are you trying to send me up, *signorina*?'

'No, of course I'm not!' she gasped, appalled that
he could suspect her of being so ill-mannered.

The grip on her elbow as he wove her in and out
of the market place was sufficiently punishing to
cast doubt upon whether he had believed her. Impatience echoed in his footsteps as he guided her
through a labyrinth of streets, not speaking until
they rounded a corner where he halted to indicate
with a nod of his head.

'You recognise this piazza?' Seeming pleased with
her brief nod, he added: 'Good, then you will have
no difficulty finding your grandfather's house.
Arrivederci once again, Signorina Rossi!'

He had turned on his heel and disappeared before Rosalba had time to gather up sufficient courage to put to him the questions that were burning on her lips. Questions such as: How do you know that Conte Rossi is my grandfather? How come you are aware that I'm staying in this piazza? And most curious of all: Why have you been following me? For how could he have known about the incident at the fruit stall and been close enough to rescue her from the bag-snatcher other than by keeping her under close observation?

To her intense relief she discovered that her grandfather's house was as silent and isolated as it had been when she left it. She sped through the hall and along the passageways, then when she had gained the safety of her room collapsed panting on to the bed feeling she had been closer to danger than at any other period in her lifetime. The stranger, whoever he was, had a terrifying effect upon her nerves. Many times Aprile had used the word 'machismo' when enthusing about the attractions of Mediterranean men, but she had never felt curious enough to ask her cousin to explain its meaning. Yet now she somehow sensed that whatever it was the word represented the stranger possessed it in abundance. Her mind groped. It had nothing to do with being tall, dark and handsome, for she had met a few such men and they had left her cold, nor was it entirely connected with powerful physique, self-assurance or charm. 'Machismo', she decided nervously, was an inner attribute, probably an inherited trait, that had nothing to do with physical appearance and everything to do with the art of being a man ...

CHAPTER FOUR

THEY dined late that evening—nine-thirty, the time at which Rosalba was usually nibbling a couple of biscuits and drinking a cup of cocoa before retiring to bed. She was not the least bit tired and she had eaten next to nothing since leaving home, yet her stomach revolted against the mound of pasta Rita heaped upon her plate.

'Oh, that's far too much! One spoonful will do, thank you, Rita.'

'Nonsense!' her grandfather intervened just as Rita was about to remove the heaped-up plate. 'Rita's lasagne is delicious—eat it up, it will do you good. I have heard it said,' his pebble-hard eyes roved her slight, shrinking frame, 'that the English do not eat, and your frailty, *nipotina*, would seem to bear this out. One cannot converse, relax, or sleep well if one has not dined well.' With a lift of an eyebrow he indicated to Rita that she should replace the heaped-up plate before concluding: 'We will talk after we have eaten; a hungry stomach has no ears.'

Whereas Aprile would have argued that food lacking the sauce of hunger is tasteless, Rosalba was so petrified by the Conte's autocratic manner that she immediately dug her fork into a small portion of pasta filled with minced meat and dripping with sauce and transferred it to her mouth, suppressing a shudder as it slid across her tongue and down her throat. She had never been fond of pasta, it was a dish that had seldom been served at home, and yet she knew it well because her Aunt Caterina had over the years dished it up in all of its variations. In order not to offend her aunt she had waded through plates of ravioli, tortellini, cannelloni, spaghetti and fettuccine until eventually familiarity had bred a tolerant acceptance of the Italian favourite which, according to legend, had been one of the unusual, exotic items the intrepid Marco Polo had imported into Italy from the mysterious Orient. As she struggled valiantly to make headway into the pile upon her plate, conscious of her grandfather's alert eyes, she decided there and then that pasta was a dish she disliked intensely.

Aprile had been watching her cousin with amusement, an amusement that gave way to pity. To Rosalba's relief, she launched into witty conversation with their grandfather, hoping to distract his attention from the girl whose meek obedience had not, as Aprile had feared, elicited purring approval but seemed to be goading the suave Conte into an uncharacteristic betrayal of irritation. Basically, Aprile decided, once she had succeeded in smoothing his ruffled feathers, the old man was a fighter, one who thrives on opposition, which was why Rosalba's gentleness had left him floundering. To him, she was as a first sip of milk after a diet of champagne.

She smiled, supposedly in response to her grandfather's quip, but in reality her amusement came from within. She had dreaded the thought of

Rosalba usurping her position in the old man's affections, but she need not have worried, it was becoming obvious that the two were as compatible as a lettuce and a rabbit.

With her grandfather's attention occupied Rosalba was able to bluff her way through the main course by spreading salad thinly over her plate. As meticulously her grandfather mixed his own salad dressing, pouring exact amounts of olive oil, red wine vinegar, salt and pepper that had been set near to hand, he jerked her to attention with the sudden enquiry:

'Are you feeling quite refreshed, or are you too tired to enjoy what I am sure you will consider a treat?' He glanced first at Aprile whose sparkling eyes and animated expression were answer enough, then turned enquiring eyes upon Rosalba, who blushed with fright and forced an inchoerent stammer.

'Yes ... no ... That is ... I mean ...'

'She's perfectly willing to do anything that's asked of her,' Aprile came to her rescue. 'Rosalba is happy to leave the making of decisions to others.'

Disappointment and a hint of distaste flickered across her grandfather's face before, with a shrug of his shoulders, he dismissed Rosalba completely and directed his next remark to Aprile. 'Can I take it, then, that you will not be averse to visiting a fashion show that is to be held this evening in the Palazzo Armerina, the home of a friend of mine who, when she heard of your visit, insisted that I buy tickets for the show which is being held in aid of some charity or other? Most of the leading fashion houses will be represented and as it is an expensive business transporting stock, sets and models by air, the Princess Armerina has made it plain that she expects all whom she has invited to place many orders.'

He stared hard, and as their eyes collided they exchanged a glance of mutual understanding, a silent indication from the Conte that his promise was about to be fulfilled and instant recognition by Aprile that, as a reward for services rendered, she was being given *carte blanche* to order whatever outfits took her fancy.

That the exchange had gone way beyond Rosalba's head was evident to her grandfather when, as he slewed a look of interrogation across the width of the table, she jerked upright as if bitten, and forced a timid smile. It was clear that the labels of leading fashion houses meant less than nothing to her.

'Who is your favourite designer, my dear?' he shot, eyeing her printed cotton dress with curiosity.

'She hasn't one,' Aprile trilled. 'She makes all her own dresses, Nonno, as I'm sure you've noticed!'

The effect upon Rosalba of their amused sarcasm was a stricken look that pierced the shell around her grandfather's heart. 'Yet still she manages to look unusually lovely,' he soothed. 'You, my dear Aprile, are blessed with flair, you could dare to knot a sweater around your hips, shop for clothes in a flea market, dine out in a sack, if ever you should feel so inclined, and yet end up being complimented upon your individual style. Your cousin, on the other hand, has a personality that cries out for superb luxury clothes. I have an urge to see her dressed in a calm little Givenchy suit or, better still, a classic Scherrer dress that would complement her serene beauty.'

Aprile gave a peal of astonished laughter. 'But you can't call that fashion any longer, Nonno! In the world of haute couture there are still a few stubborn eccentrics, such as those you've just mentioned, who obstinately continue to design clothes of boring, unoriginal elegance, ageing bastions who refuse to recognise that the world around them has changed and that to star in fashion today one needs to be sharp, trendy and way-out.'

'Way-out ...!' He threw up his hands in horror. 'The phrase is meaningless to me. No!' he silenced her when she made to interrupt, 'do not attempt to explain, for I'm quite certain I should find the meaning every bit as distasteful as the expression itself.' He rose from the table, his frame incredibly upright in spite of his age, and instructed, 'If you girls have quite finished I'll ring for the chauffeur to fetch the car.'

They left him to go to their rooms in search of wraps, Aprile almost dancing along the passageway in her excitement, with Rosalba following laggardly in her wake. In less than five seconds Aprile had shrugged into a long black cloak lined with the same shimmering green silk as her dress and dashed into Rosalba's room where she found her sitting on a stool in front of her dressing table plucking nervously at a filmy woollen stole.

'Are you ready?' she urged brightly, determined to ignore obvious signs of reluctance.

Rosalba cleared her throat, conscious that Aprile

suspected what she was about to say and was already marshalling her arguments. 'Do you think Grandfather would mind very much if I asked to be excused?'

'If you opt out, you mean,' Aprile corrected coldly. 'Yes, I'm sure he would mind—in fact, he would be furious. Fashion shows aren't exactly his scene, yet he's prepared to suffer the experience simply to give us pleasure. It would be cruel to snub him by refusing to go.'

As usual, she chose her words well, directing accusing barbs that set her cousin's conscience writhing.

Stabbed by a remorse that felt almost physical, Rosalba jumped to her feet and flung the stole around her shoulders. 'You're right, I am being selfish,' she admitted, her cheeks pink with shame. 'Of course I must go.'

Ten minutes later the car drew up in front of a floodlit *palazzo* showing a crush of shadowy figures outlined against the ground floor windows. Loud music spilled out into the street each time the massive front door was opened to admit guests still pouring out of cars parked down the length of adjoining streets and from taxis pulling up every few seconds outside the imposing façade.

When they were shown into a colossal room crammed to overflowing with an argumentative, protesting, gossiping, chattering, speculative crowd Rosalba gasped with horror. As they entered, the mass parted to make way for the imposing Conte and his dark, exotic butterfly of a granddaughter, then immediately closed behind them leaving

Rosalba stranded, a fluttering silver moth cast into the shadows. She cried out, but the sound was drowned by a crash of music. Then lights were lowered, spotlights blazed, and hundreds of cameras began flashing as model girls began stepping out on to a makeshift stage, pranced along a catwalk, then gyrated in time with the music to show every detail of their outfits before retreating offstage to make a quick change.

She struggled into a corner, then stood with her back pressed against a wall gazing wide-eyed at a spectacle that was completely new and alien to her. The accompanying music was a harsh, ear-shattering cacophony of noise that set her teeth on edge and drove her to search, wide-eyed with desperation, for an avenue of escape. But she was surrounded, cut off from the only exit by a crush of late arrivals all eagerly pressing forward to gain a better view, yet many of them still overspilling into the hallway beyond.

Resigned to the inevitability of remaining where she was until the show had ended, she pushed her fingers into her ears to deaden the noise and stared with disbelieving eyes as the show developed into a spectacle, the models titillating the male section of the audience with glimpses of bare breast through see-through fabrics, flaunted buttocks, and skirts slashed to reveal long, slender thighs.

The clothes themselves were grotesque, she decided, deliberately distorted and exaggerated in order to achieve maximum visual impact, reducing the girls who wore them to the status of a Folies Bergère chorus line. When a model sauntered into the centre of the stage wearing an outfit with shoulders padded out to the width of a 250-lb wrestler Rosalba tried unsuccessfully to suppress a gasp. A woman in front of her turned round to smile.

'Don't worry, my dear. In the shops Montana's shoulders won't be anything like as wide,' she reassured her, then continued with the confidence of one who knows the fashion world inside out: 'Colours and prints are chosen for catwalk impact; actual design or cut is irrelevant, only the message is important.'

As the woman spoke, Rosalba had politely removed her fingers from her ears and she was just about to replace them when the music was rent by the ear-splitting roar of a motor cycle amplified to represent the noise of a hundred or more, a fanfare for the slim coloured model who leapt on to the stage wearing skin-tight, smooth black leathers. A wave of cheers, catcalls and whistles greeted her entrance, and as the excruciating din continued Rosalba fought for breath in the stifling room and felt herself sliding lower and lower down the supporting wall, her distressed state going unnoticed in a sea of waving arms.

She had almost given up the struggle to breathe and had begun a slow slide into oblivion when arms grasped her waist and she felt herself being lifted roughly yet securely while a harsh voice commanded the crowd around them to give way. She must have lost consciousness for a while, because her next recollection was of gulping in air fresh as the sparkle of wine that was brushing a cool, perfume-laden caress across her skin.

When her senses stopped whirling she focused upon a huge moon grinning down from above dark tree-tops, heard the tinkling of a nearby fountain and saw waxen petals strewn where they had fallen on the path beneath her feet. Then, as she shifted slightly on a hard, uncomfortable seat, she realised that she was in a garden at the rear of the *palazzo* and that she was not alone. Sitting next to her, immobile, unfriendly and stern, was a figure bathed in moonlight that highlighted the bitter twist of his mouth and eyes that were smouldering furnaces of frustration.

'*You* again ... !' she addressed the dark stranger, feeling confused but not surprised. Then, still light-headed, she surprised herself with the observation: 'You're like a hawk, *signore*, always hovering. Are you my self-elected protector?'

'A hawk does not protect, *signorina*,' he told her in a flat monotone which nevertheless managed to convey inward furore. 'Its function is to hunt, to pounce, and then to destroy.'

Though the night was balmy, she shuddered. There was menace in his tone and a contempt she found upsetting. She was used to being ignored, but not disliked.

'Er ... thank you once again for rescuing me.' She tugged her stole closer around her shoulders. 'You needn't wait, I'm feeling all right now. Please don't miss the rest of the show on my account.'

His short, hard laugh grated in her ears. 'Do I look the sort of man,' he mocked, 'who needs to seek his pleasures in stuffy, overcrowded rooms watching grotesquely-dressed females parading half naked before men made pallid and bloated by too much easy living? They drain our country of its wealth, these morons, and give nothing in return. As profits accumulate the financial power of the city men increases, so much so that they become the source of ready money for much of Europe, yet in our poorer regions peasants are still scratching a living from the ground using the same implements as their fathers and their grandfathers before them—their bare hands! In the north they have tractors, but here in the south even horses are scarce and it is a donkey that carries hay to the barns, grapes to the wine press and its owner to market. Houses and shops are dilapidated, there is little cash, people are poor, their possessions mostly handmade and crude—a peasant owning a bicycle is considered to be a man of means—and yet women such as yourself think nothing of spending thousands of lire on hideous garments such as those being shown tonight!'

She stared at him, her eyes dark blue and wide. His tall frame, muscular yet slim, seemed quite at home in a dinner jacket tailored to sit perfectly upon broad shoulders, his evening shirt, ruffled down the front and at the cuffs, was of a quality that would have found favour with even her fastidious grandfather. Brown hands, capable, yet with nails scrupulously manicured, betrayed him a stranger to manual labour, yet his words, his tone of ragged impatience, rang with resentment of his surroundings and allegiance to the peasantry he had so proudly extolled.

Rosalba said the first thing that popped into her head.

'Are you a communist, *signore*?'

His head jerked erect. She felt fluttering panic as his eyes pinned her like a moth within his angry stare. Then to her relief she saw anger drain from him until all that remained was a contempt that made her squirm.

'No, I am merely a humanitarian who grows impatient with the wealthy because of their greed and because of their blindness to the poverty that is all around them. Improvement will come—*must come*, I tell myself—yet patience is not one of my virtues. Whatever I want I must have immediately—I deplore the fact that waiting has become one of our national pastimes.'

Whatever I want I must have immediately! She believed him. Everything about his coiled-spring frame, out-thrust jaw, impatient mouth and fierce eyes indicated that here was a man who found conventions irritating, a bandit who, if he was not given, would recklessly take!

Suddenly she began to tremble. She felt afraid, afraid of the cross-currents she sensed seething beneath the controlled calm of the man who, since her arrival in his country, had attached himself as close as an avenging shadow. She was afraid, also, of the country itself, a land that needed a mere scratch upon its surface to release a volcanic eruption of fiery emotions. Reminded of the pledge she had made to fight her inherent cowardice, she mastered her voice sufficiently to croak:

'Why are you so interested in my movements? Don't deny that you are,' she stumbled in her haste. 'Obviously you've set out to discover all you can about me—the fact that I'm Conte Rossi's grand-daughter, the place where I'm staying. I'm grateful, of course, that you came to my rescue in the market place and again this evening, but nevertheless, your presence in both places indicates a knowledge of my movements that can't be explained away as coin-cidence. Why me?' she pleaded, her blue eyes enormous with puzzlement. 'I could understand your being interested in my cousin, Aprile, because all men are, but I'm nondescript—so *ordinary*!'

Again he laughed, the harsh sound she had begun to associate with him. '*Nondescript! Ordinary!* If it suits you to pretend to be what you are not then con-tinue to do so, but do not underestimate my intel-ligence by believing me fooled by your game. You are Rosalba, daughter of Angelo, granddaughter of Conte Pietro Rossi de Città del Monte,' he astounded her by saying, 'therefore to me you are the most important person in the world. I've longed for you to arrive so that the burden of duty may be eased from my shoulders. Now that you are at last here is it not understandable that I should wish to keep you always within my sight? *Arrivederci!*' he stood up to sketch a smart salute, 'until our next meeting, which I promise will be soon. You, English dove, are the instrument for which I have waited— the bait I will use to tempt the snake out of his pit!'

CHAPTER FIVE

FIVE minutes later Aprile discovered Rosalba standing exactly where the stranger had left her, motionless as a statue, speechless with fear.

'There you are!' Her nonchalant tone penetrated Rosalba's frozen stupor. 'I've looked everywhere for you. I knew you weren't keen on the fashion show,' she scolded crossly, 'but I didn't dream you'd go so far as to walk out on us! Grandfather was so annoyed he almost didn't buy you a thing, but I talked him round. Not only that!' she enthused, catching Rosalba by the elbow to drag her along the path leading towards the *palazzo*, 'I've managed to persuade some of the designers to let us buy outfits that were actually modelled this evening! This show is the last of the season, so when I explained that we're to be here for only two weeks and are desperately short of fashionable clothes they agreed to sell. Grandfather helped, of course, by waving his cheque book under their noses,' she chuckled gleefully. Then becoming aware of her cousin's lack of enthusiasm, she stopped so suddenly that Rosalba cannoned into her. 'What does it take to get you excited?' she exploded. 'I feel as if I'm dragging an anchor. Hurry up, *do*, I can't wait to try on those fabulous creations!'

'*Aprile!*' At last Rosalba won the struggle to find her voice. 'Stop for a minute and listen, I have something very important to tell you!'

Aprile's eyebrows shot skywards, but she contained her impatience, realising only then that her cousins was really upset.

'I ... I don't know how to begin,' Rosalba stammered. 'There's a man—one who looks like a bandit —who's been following me ever since I arrived here, and tonight ... tonight, he said ... he threatened ... Oh, I don't know *exactly* what he threatened, but I'm sure he's dangerous!'

'Dangerous to whom?' Aprile sounded as if she were humouring a child. Pushing Rosalba down on to a seat, she laid the palm of her hand on her brow. 'Are you feeling feverish?' she frowned.

When Rosalba shook her head Aprile put an arm around her shoulders and with a show of aggravating indulgence proceeded to coax: 'Sit there and don't move while I go for Grandfather; I think you're delirious and in need of a doctor. I'll be gone only a few minutes, so don't be afraid—I assure you there are no longer any bandits in Sicily, and if you had been followed, as you suspect, someone would have noticed, because you haven't been alone once since our arrival. So please don't worry,' she gave her a quick squeeze, 'you're in absolutely no danger.'

Rosalba's despairing eyes followed Aprile's retreating back as she sped along the path leading to the *palazzo*. She could hardly blame her for jumping to the conclusion that illness was the cause of her wild accusations, for she had not repeated any of the conversation she had had with the stranger, nor had she mentioned the escapade in the market place.

It was also evident that the small commotion she had caused when she fainted had gone mostly unnoticed. It was hardly surprising, therefore, that Aprile should conclude that her incoherent warning was the result of some virulent attack of fever.

She felt it useless to utter a protest or to attempt any further explanation when her grandfather arrived accompanied by his chauffeur and an anxious Aprile who could be heard long before she was seen explaining to the Conte.

'She was babbling some nonsense about bandits, and being followed,' Rosalba overheard her telling him as they hurried towards her. 'Her eyes were staring—sort of vacant—and she was shivering, although when I touched her she felt hot.'

The Conte wasted no time with questions but instructed the chauffeur: 'Alessandro, carry the child to the car, drive straight home and tell Rita she is to be put straight to bed.'

'No, Grandfather, there's no need!' Rosalba protested. 'I'm quite capable of walking to the car.'

'You will do as you are told!' he thundered, forgetting for the moment that she was supposedly ill. He apologised immediately: 'I'm sorry, my dear, but I am worried about you, so worried that I will not rest until you have been seen by my own doctor who will be along just as soon as I can get in touch with him—he'll come, even if I have to get him out of bed.'

Appalled by the thought, she tried a further protest. 'I wish you'd believe me when I tell you there's nothing wrong with me! What I told Aprile is the truth, every word of it—I *have* been followed by a man ever since I set foot in Sicily. He carried me out of the *palazzo* tonight when I fainted, and here in this very garden he threatened to ... to ...'

'To do what ...?' he urged narrowly, better aware than Aprile that in this land of fiery passions anything is possible.

'I'm not sure exactly ...'

'Ah!' His face cleared, then once more adopted lines of worry. 'Take her home, Alessandro,' he instructed crisply, 'and hurry!'

The doctor confirmed as Rosalba knew he would, that there was nothing wrong that a good night's sleep would not put right. 'It is the travelling, the excitement,' he tut-tutted. 'You have had a very long day, *signorina*, and you are not yet acclimatised to our hot weather. Take things easy for a while, and when you are out of doors remember always to wear a hat.'

Wear a hat! Rosalba's pale, solemn face reflected none of the panic she was feeling. It was not protection from the sun that she needed but protection from the barbarous hints and coolly worded threats of the man who appeared out of nowhere with the suddenness and stealth of an apparition.

Was he a figment of her imagination? she began to wonder, scanning the faces ranged around her bed. Aprile, her grandfather, the doctor, had all tried to convince her that he did not exist. Then with certainty she knew that they were wrong. Apparitions did not possess sinewy fingers that could grasp as tightly as his had done—even now she could feel the impression where his fingers had snapped a bracelet of steel around her wrist!

They set out for Città del Monte after breakfast the next morning. Alessandro seemed perplexed by the pile of extra luggage that had to be accommodated in the boot of the car and confessed himself beaten when, after a fruitless half hour of packing and rearranging, there was still one large suitcase for which he could find no room.

'But we must take that one!' Aprile wailed. 'It contains the outfits I bought at the show. Put it in the back of the car, Alessandro, it will fit in easily if my cousin and I sit either side of it.'

Conversation was desultory as they made their way out of the capital, until by the time the car was speeding away from the outskirts it was entirely non-existent. The Conte seemed deeply preoccupied.

Aprile did not bother even to glance out of the window, but sat smiling secretly as if consumed by some inner excitement. Rosalba was glad of the chance to observe without distraction her first glimpse of a country that was new to her and yet looked strangely familiar. Ochre-coloured stone, miles upon miles of vineyards, fields of melons ripening in the sun were reality, whereas home had become a blurred memory.

They passed through small towns and villages, streets of pink, blue and green-washed houses combined into a joyful riot of colour made all the more glorious by the gaiety of brilliant sunshine. Soon flower-carpeted valleys gave way to slopes barren except for masses of starry-blossomed asphodel. On a stark mountainside, alone except for sheep and goats struggling to find food among prickly pears, cacti and scrub, she saw a temple rearing high, a perfection of golden stone projecting an aura of timeless serenity.

The road began to incline steeply as they approached a forest of tall pines which, as they plunged inside it, enclosed them within a cool green mantle and filled the car with pungent aroma. As the road spiralled up the mountainside in ever-decreasing circles Rosalba perched on the edge of her seat, eager to drink in every sight exposed as they rounded numerous twists and turns. When, still climbing, they emerged from the forest she saw far below a wide coastal plain with glistening saltings and windmills; the Spanish towers and rooftops of a town spread around a sickle-shaped harbour, and far out to sea a scattering of tiny islands.

'Not long now—look, child, the village is in sight.' Her grandfather's words sent her eyes slewing ahead and she gasped with delight as the car passed beneath a gateway of silver-grey granite with walls of the same stone enclosing a settlement of ancient dwellings perched high upon the mountain top.

Obligingly, Alessandro slowed down as they progressed along narrow streets without footpaths, paved with the same silver stone that had been used for the fortifications. Rosalba caught glimpses of flower-crammed courtyards with outside staircases trailing ivy down every step, and a small central square with a *trattoria* where tables and chairs were arranged outside to attract passing customers.

They then entered a tree-lined drive cutting through extensive gardens that widened with the suddenness of sun piercing cloud to expose a medieval castle that seemed gouged out of silver-grey granite.

'Magnificent!' she breathed.

'You like it?' For the first time the Conte looked genuinely pleased.

'It's overwhelming, Grandfather. Too much to take in all at once!'

'There's no hurry,' he smiled as he helped her out of the car. 'You are young, you are a Rossi, and this is your home.'

Too bemused to pay much attention to his words, she allowed him to lead her up a flight of steps, through archways supported by many stone pillars, then into a hall so high she had to tip back her head in order to encompass the full extent of a ceiling made up of crisscrossed beams, each intricately carved and painted. Splendid chandeliers, all crystal and gold and silver metal, were suspended, one in each of four corners, like gigantic spiders waiting to descend. Oil paintings lined the walls, interspersed with shadowed niches holding statues with cold marble expressions that seemed to project indifference as to whether they were examined or overlooked.

Visibly amused by her awestricken expression, the Conte took her by the arm to lead her up a flight of stairs with treads of the same silver stone but with balusters of pure porcelain that rang—as he demonstrated by striking each with a fingernail as he passed—with a different note. He opened the first doorway of many ranged around the first-floor landing and watched closely for her reaction to the room that he had chosen especially for her.

He had noted that she was a creature of few words, yet all the gratitude he could have wished for was present in her voice when she stepped inside, stood stock-still, then whispered.

'*Oh, Grandfather* ...!'

The background colour predominating was pale blue on walls, ceiling and doors, but superimposed upon each surface, curved and scrolled in vivid colours, were panels painted with slim flowering trees that had branches supporting unidentifiable birds of exotic plumage. A huge fourposter bed had hangings embroidered with the same design in coloured wools, and set upon a pale blue, thick piled carpet were onyx-topped tables on ornate gilt legs, a multi-mirrored dressing-table holding a crystal vase massed with blue and white flowers, dainty spindle-legged chairs and a couch covered in the same hand embroidered cloth as the bed hangings. Next to it, a small table supported a porcelain lamp-stand topped with a pleated cream shade.

'Well, my dear,' her grandfather urged softly, 'do you approve?'

She swung to face him, her eyes wide, her lips formed into a round, pink 'oh' of surprise, but no words came.

He smiled the inscrutable smile of a man unwilling to betray too much satisfaction.

'I'll leave you to settle in,' he patted her shoulder, 'but as we have not yet had time to talk, it would please me very much if you would meet me downstairs in my study as soon as you are ready. Shall we say in half an hour ...?' He waited until she nodded, then stepped outside, closing the door behind him.

Rosalba remained in the middle of the room staring at the beauty all around her yet conscious of an undefinable fear, a feeling that all was not as it should be. In such airy, sunlit surroundings she should have been feeling as free as a bird. Instead, she fixed worried eyes upon the feathered images painted upon the walls, fighting a dawning suspicion that she might one day be as they were—trapped until eternity within an impregnable castle!

Rita had been transported to the castle earlier that morning to supervise the staff and otherwise prepare for their stay. Rosalba met her in the great hall when half an hour later she went downstairs in search of her grandfather.

'Which is Grandfather's study, Rita?' she wavered, confronted by many tall double doors with ornamental grilles protecting half their height.

'The Conte has changed his mind, *signorina*. As the day is so warm he has decided that you will be more comfortable in the loggia. Come with me, I'll show you the way.'

She followed Rita and stepped outside on to a wide veranda lined with archways opening out into a courtyard. It was furnished with a harmonious blend of rush matting and comfortably upholstered cane furniture. As she entered her grandfather rose to meet her.

'Sit here, *nipotina*.' He ushered her towards a settee, then when he was certain she was comfortable sat down beside her. 'At last we have found time to talk.' His tight mouth relaxed into a smile. 'But you look tense, my dear. Sit quietly for a moment and listen to the music of the fountains. There are seven of them, each representing a century of Rossi ownership. The next one is due to be erected next year and I should like you to be the one to choose its design.'

'I ...? Her whisper was barely audible above the sound of water cascading down circular pyramids of stone; tinkling from the flutes of Pan; gushing from the mouths of grinning gargoyles; being spat with force from the innards of stone fish and seeping from the eyes of marble cherubs. The whole courtyard around which the seven fountains were set seemed to her sensitive soul to pulsate with the sound of sighing and weeping.

'Yes, my dear.' When her grandfather's papery-skinned hand enclosed hers she almost jerked away. 'That is what I want to discuss with you. The fact that you are my heir, the only living Rossi who bears my name, and that everything you see around you is your heritage—your birthright. My insistence that Aprile should bring you here was no mere whim.'

Rosalba recoiled from this confirmation of her cousin's duplicity. Her mother had suspected an ulterior motive, but she had been unable to believe that the fondness she felt for her cousin was not reciprocated. The realisation that Aprile had used her was unbearably painful ...

'You will, of course, have to take up residence here,' she caught up again the thread of her grandfather's words.

'I couldn't do that,' she jerked. 'Mother would never agree to give up her home.'

'There is no place here for your mother.' As the chill of his voice reached out across the courtyard the very waters of the fountains seemed to fall silent during a frozen pause. Then dismissing her mother completely, he continued in a calm reasonable manner which was nevertheless belied by the imperious drumming of his fingers against cane. 'Your father was my only son. Regrettably, after he was born my wife was told that she could never bear another child, so, as you can imagine, he was very important to me.'

When Rosalba choked back impulsive words he inclined his head, as if acknowledging her right to doubt, and explained carefully: 'I'm sure you are aware of the rift that developed between your father and myself—a rift that was not of my making, but one which I tried many times to bridge. I blame outside influences for the fact that my son rebuffed all the advances I made towards him.'

'Are you implying that my mother——'

'I never imply, I state facts,' he silenced her. 'But we will not argue on that point, your father's death has made it irrelevant. I can, however, speak with authority when I say that your father was a good son, a man very conscious of his responsibilities, one who, if he had been given the chance, would have made a fitting successor to myself and to the many notable Rossis who have gone before us. You see, my dear, I knew him as you did not. All his life, from infancy, through boyhood and adolescence, he was trained in the ways of nobility. I insisted upon him working in the fields with his people, but only because it was necessary for him to get to know them well and for them to respect him not just as a future Conte but as a man who would ask of them nothing that he could not do himself. The mantle of leadership can be a burden—which is why he was made to don it at a very early age in order that, as the years progressed, he would become accustomed to its weight. Through no wish of his own,' his voice suddenly grated, 'that mantle was torn from his shoulders.'

Rosalba felt the impact of his pebble-hard eyes upon her face, but when she looked up she sensed that he was not looking at her but down the avenues of the past. Obviously, what he saw there did not please him. She dared not interrupt, for she knew that he was not yet finished. Words seemed dragged from him when with difficulty he hauled his mind back into the present.

'I have never been able to imagine my son as a shopkeeper, so I realise that it must be equally hard for you to picture him here among his own people, resolving their grievances, sharing their laughter, mingling his tears with theirs. It is *shameful*,' when his clenched fist connected with his palm she jerked with shock and dug tense fingers into the cane armrest of the settee, 'shameful that he should have been so deprived of his heritage by a mere *woman*!'

The venom in his voice turned Rosalba's stomach. Suddenly his motives became clear as the ugly word vendetta reared its head. He had not brought her here because of love of his son, nor because he needed her to take his place, but because he wanted to be revenged upon her mother. Over the years he had nursed resentment like a festering sore, hating her for depriving him first of a son and then of a daughter. She recoiled from the thought, yet as she was pinned by his fanatical gleam she felt her suspicions confirmed.

Her horrified eyes must have warned him that he had betrayed too much too soon. Calling upon massive strength of will, he managed to control his wrath, forcing his hard expression into lines of sorrowful regret. His placating tone held apology for frightening her.

'I'm sorry, my dear, for allowing my emotions to run away with me—please, I beg you, try to make allowances for old age.' She braced herself for an assault upon her sympathy. 'Old trees,' he played mournfully on her emotions 'grow stronger, old rivers grow wider, but old men merely grow lonely. Stay with me, Rosalba,' his voice strengthened as with masterly pretence he urged: 'I know your father would have wished it. His blood runs in your veins, his nature lurks deep within you—through you he could live again!'

CHAPTER SIX

For the rest of that day Rosalba kept well out of her grandfather's way, losing herself in grounds that were to some extent cultivated yet had a wildness that suggested that nature had done most and man least. The castle was built of stone, but had a liquid core of water—water used not only for drinking, swimming or washing but also as a sound, as a reflector of light, and as a diversion. She traced its source from a spring gushing out of the mountainside and followed its course to a reservoir teeming with fish and shaded by ancient trees, lost it when it plunged underground, then discovered it emerging once more as a waterfall at the very top of the sloping gardens. From there it linked a chain of fountains set in gardens so steeply stepped that no mechanical aids were necessary to force water that had flowed under its own natural momentum day after day, year after year, century after century.

Its music was soothing to her feverish mind and as she followed its passage over mellowed stone, beneath the shade of weeping trees, watched it fall in light beards against harsh rock, disperse into individual jets and fans, then come together once more into a single thick, urgent outpouring, she gradually began to regain some of her usual serenity.

After wandering for hours she sat down on the rim of a fountain. Two great river gods, the Tiber and the Arno, were imprisoned in stone beneath gushing water, each wearing a chiselled, stony expression of indifference to the other, their lichen-stained heads turned aside as if refusing in perpetuity to acknowledge each other.

She sighed, wondering why, in a land of such beauty, everyone should be so obsessed with pride—expressions pictured it, eyes mirrored it, words and gestures rang with the vice so integral to the Sicilian race it was perpetuated even in the stone images of their dead.

'Tell me,' she addressed Arno whose watered visage looked the least intimidating of the two, 'how can I escape? It seems ridiculous, in this age of freedom of the individual, to suspect that my grandfather will try to keep me here against my will, yet you and I both know that here in his mountain fortress the Conte has kept alive the world of centuries past wherein each Rossi was king, every Rossi wish a command. To attempt to reason with him would be useless, to argue would be unwise, so I have no choice but to resort to stealth. I think I shall keep a low profile for a few days,' she confided in the granite features that centuries of water-massage had failed to soften, 'hoping for inspiration. I'll think of something—*I must*,' her voice developed a wild, ragged edge, 'otherwise I'll finish up joining my grandfather's collection of mute, mindless mummies!'

She avoided the trauma of accompanying her grandfather and Aprile to dinner by pleading a headache. That her excuse had been accepted without question was proved when Rita entered her bedroom carrying a tray.

'I've brought you a little light supper, *signorina*,' she smiled, setting the tray upon a table. 'The Conte sends his condolences but adds that he is pleased at your wisdom in following the doctor's advice to take things easy. I will return to collect the tray later. Once this has been done you are to be left undisturbed.'

In order to allay any concern about her lack of appetite, Rosalba ate as much of the fluffy omelette as she could manage and drank a glass of wine. Then she undressed and donned cool pyjamas before slipping into bed, her enjoyment of silken sheets intensified by the contrasting serviceable cotton. For a while she dozed, her sleep light enough for her to register the sound of Rita's footfalls as she crept into the room to collect the supper tray, then tiptoed out again. From under drowsy lids she watched curtains billowing in a breeze filtering softly through an open window, then as a pale sickle of moon glided behind clouds and the room darkened she closed her eyes and surrendered to deep dreamless sleep.

Much later, at an hour when the castle and its occupants were wrapped in brooding silence, she awoke with a start and saw a dark, menacing shadow advancing towards her. A sharp, confused gasp was all she managed before a hand closed over her mouth and determined words were hissed against her ear.

'Don't be foolish, *signorina*. If you remain silent you will come to no harm, but otherwise ...!' The bedcovers were whipped back and an arm reached out to haul her roughly from the bed. The hand was withdrawn from her mouth to be replaced immediately by a gag that was thrust between her lips and kept anchored by a strip of cloth tied tightly behind her head. An hysterical scream rose into her throat but was blocked by the constricting gag as she was lifted, thrown like a sack of potatoes over a broad shoulder, and carried on to the balcony outside her room. Sky, earth and granite walls combined into a whirling kaleidoscope when with an ease possessed by only the very strong and the superbly fit, her abductor swung first one leg and then the other over the balcony and began to descend walls massed with centuries' growth of creeper, feeling carefully for footholds among tangled shoots, working his way foot by foot, hand by hand, seemingly indifferent to the fate of the bundle of humanity gripping talons of terror into his back.

When eventually the horrific descent was concluded, he set her down upon her feet, but found it impossible to dislodge her choking arms from around his neck. She heard him chuckle, but would not be shamed into releasing him, not until with breathtaking impudence he murmured, 'Careful, *signorina*, your attachment verges on the provocative, and as I am far from being a member of some sub-species devoid of feelings your passionate clinging is playing havoc with my emotions.'

His mocking sarcasm had an effect similar to that of a slap across the face. With flaming cheeks Rosalba jerked away, leaving a yard of space between them. She was glad of the darkness, grateful that it hid from full view her shivering, inadequately clothed body. To her surprise, he did not immediately pounce to reclaim her and it was some seconds before she realised that she was alone, his dark shadow no longer looming over her in the darkness.

She had only just gathered her wits sufficiently to take her first fleeing steps when there was a thump at her feet, followed by a dark form that sprang from a height and landed, rocking on his heels, next to her.

'You will need clothes!' He indicated with a nod the suitcase he had retrieved from her bedroom.

She stared, her eyes enormous above the tightly wound cloth that held her gag secure. She was unable to speak, but even if she had been able to she was far too shy, too inadequate with words to express her deepest fears. This was the man against whom she had tried to warn her grandfather and Aprile, the man she had likened to a bandit because of his heated views and the reckless intent she had sensed seething within him. Intent to do what? To kidnap, obviously. To him she represented the Established that he held in such contempt; he thought her privileged, and over-rich, and for this he meant to punish her. But what form would his punishment take? Would he be satisfied with depriving her of luxurious surroundings? Would he perhaps demand a ransom and kill her if it were not paid? Or did he have something much worse in mind ...?'

It was dark, yet light enough for him to read the message communicated by wide, startled eyes and a shrinking body. Stooping to pick up her suitcase, he paused before straightening to peer into her stricken face.

'What you have in mind would be very pleasant, *signorina*,' he mocked dryly, 'but much as I would like to accommodate you, at the moment we simply do not have the time.'

Putting his hand upon her elbow he propelled her into the darkness. Flinty stones bit into the soles of her bare feet, but her whimpers of pain were stifled by the gag, yet even if they had not been she suspected they would have caused him no concern. When a jeep loomed out of the darkness she lost no time obeying when he ordered her into it, and sat nursing tender feet while he turned the key in the ignition and accelerated the engine into life. Before engaging gear he shrugged off his coat and flung it in her lap.

'Here, put this on. My plans do not include nursing you through a bout of pneumonia.'

She dredged minute consolation from this rough act of kindness—a man totally devoid of compassion would have left her to freeze. But then again, an inner voice warned, if ransom were his aim it would be in his best interests to keep her in good health, at least until the money had been paid.

The zig-zag descent down the mountain was an extension of the nightmare that had begun with his appearance in her room. She held on tightly as with what seemed to her maniacal speed he threw the jeep around hairpin bends and looped corners of the corkscrew road whose precipitous drops on one side and overhangs of rock on the other had been intimidating enough in daylight; darkness, and her inherent timidity, helped to magnify the hazards a thousandfold.

Her relief was tremendous when finally she sensed the road levelling out and the veil of darkness slowly lifting so that soon she was able to distinguish straggling growths of prickly pear and spiky sisal leaning out over the road, their silhouettes looking eerily human; giant hands beckoning them onward or enormous feet grotesquely poking through a hedge. The mountain housing the Castle of Fountains was far behind them by the time the sun began inching over the horizon. Olive groves, orchards, vines and bamboo thickets stretched either side of a road heading straight towards a wall of mountains. Frozen, both mentally and physically, she remained still and quiet. A couple of hours had passed by the time they began ascending one of the peaks etched like jagged teeth against a brilliant blue sky, the road winding through a wilderness of bare limestone, the lower slopes terraced for cultivation, narrow, built-up steps sown with buckwheat by some poor, hardworking optimist.

As yet there was no one about, just herself and her captor driving up a grey pallid slope dotted with enormous white boulders, numerous and large enough to hide an army. When at last the protesting, whining engine seemed ready to give up the ghost the road terminated abruptly and he swung the jeep on to a plateau, heading it straight for what Rosalba thought was sheer rock face. She tensed for the impact, then slumped back in her seat when he swerved around a boulder and drove inside a huge, bare limestone cave whose dark, miserable interior intensified her misery and offered little comfort to her shivering, fear-racked body.

Obeying his curt instruction, she stumbled out of the jeep. Promptly, her legs folded beneath her and with a muttered imprecation he grabbed her by the shoulders and heaved her upright, then, using his body as a prop, he held her steady while he untied the scarf around her head. Immediately it fell loose she spat out the gag, but her mouth was too dry, her lips too tender and swollen to accommodate words.

'Welcome to our world, *signorina!*' He looked cruelly satisfied by her discomfort. 'To poverty, to hardship, to squalor—and to all the ghosts who will keep you uneasy company.'

'Who ... are ... you?' she choked painfully, fighting threatened hysteria. 'What do you want of me ...?'

'My name is Salvatore Diavolo.' He watched narrowly, seeming to expect some hint of recognition, but when her expression remained blank he continued in a voice hard with anger: 'Personally, I want nothing of you. Like myself you are a mere instrument of fate, a fate that decrees that the dead cannot rest until the ritual of custom is enacted and passion is assuaged by vengeance.'

'I'm sorry ...' Dazed and uncertain, she shook her head. 'I don't understand. Would you please explain?'

Showing impatient disbelief, he spat: 'You are a Rossi—I am a Diavolo. What further explanation is needed?'

Words did not come easy to Rosalba at the best of times, but fear and confusion drove a babbling spate from her lips.

'I am a Rossi, yes, but I've lived in England all my life, I met my grandfather for the very first time yesterday! As for your name, it means nothing to me. Why should it?'

Sunshine slanted through the cave opening and for a second she saw his ruthless expression softened by uncertainty. As his eyes probed her worried face she quailed, then, reminded of her vow to be more courageous, willed herself to weather his frowning, half-suspicious gaze.

But while he looked he, too, seemed reminded. As if some voice from the past had taken him to task, he thrust out his chest and hooked assertive thumbs into the belt with its barbaric golden buckle. That he had decided now to believe her was plain when he moved a leather-booted foot towards an upturned box and propelled it towards her, creating a noise that scraped across her tortured nerves.

'Sit, *innocente*, while I enlighten you, for I am certain the Diavolo version of the story is one that you are not familiar with. The vendetta originally arose not between the Famiglia Rossi and the Famiglia Diavolo but between Rossi and Pisciotta ...'

'*Vendetta!*' She sank down on to the box, glad of its support for her weakened limbs.

'Indeed, yes,' he mocked. 'We civilised deem ourselves a long way past savagery and in many respects we are, the most we will admit to is that our origins go back to that middle state known as barbarism, yet we Sicilians, while still laying claim to being civil-ised, are extremely sensitive to insults, and that is why the institution known as vendetta still flourishes, why it remains a necessity, for within a community where no fair and impartial authority exists a policy of reprisal is the only practicable way of preventing further outrage. In other words, *signorina*, to suffer evil similar to that which he has inflicted upon another will bring home to even a man as vindictive as your grandfather that violence does not pay in the long run.'

He paused, expecting her to argue in defence of her grandfather, but she remained silent, appalled by what she had just heard, yet suspecting that worse was yet to come. She looked away, cowed by his aggressive stance, her shrinking form swallowed by his shadow being cast by the sun rising behind him as he stood rocking on his heels at the entrance to the cave.

'Maria Pisciotta,' he continued, his voice falling harsh against her ears, 'was betrothed to one Angelo Rossi.' If possible, Rosalba became even more still. 'Arrangements had been finalised, settlements agreed, the wedding date fixed, and while Angelo was away doing service in the army Maria slaved happily until she had drawers full of sheets, pillow cases, and tablecloths all hand-sewn and em-broidered, ready for the home she was to share with Angelo when he returned. You are aware, of course, that he never did return.' The accusation was grated, an invitation to contradict, but Rosalba was not prepared to do so until she had learned all that there was to know.

'Word quickly spread that Maria had been jilted and she suffered the inevitable consequence of being regarded as a woman dishonoured, an object of pity and scorn. Then Diavolo appeared on the scene!' He moved so quickly that the sunshine slanted across her face, forcing her to blink rapidly. 'He had loved her from afar, but had remained silent because he knew that her infatuation for Angelo was so strong that to speak would have been to invite rebuff. She did not hesitate to accept, however, when he proposed marriage; to have refused would have meant her never receiving another offer, to have been condemned to spinsterhood for the rest of her life. Naturally, once Maria became his wife Diavolo joined forces with her brothers and father in the vendetta against the only remaining Rossi—the Conte. But they were mere peasants whose only skill was scratching a living from the ground and he was the all-powerful ruler of a miniature kingdom, protected always by armed bodyguards, his safety doubly assured by the inaccessibility of a fortress home patrolled day and night by an army of imported thugs whose orders were to hunt down and kill Maria's every male relative and especially her husband—Diavolo.'

'I don't believe you!' Rosalba gasped. 'Grandfather may be an autocrat, but he wouldn't kill!'

'I can assure you, *signorina*, that although he never once soiled his fingers with a knife or a gun your grandfather is responsible for the deaths of every male Pisciotta, father, sons, cousins—and other relatives so distant the relationship is hardly worth mentioning. The only ones to elude him—

but not, unfortunately, for ever—were Maria and her husband. They fled to these hills,' he hissed, 'to seek the protection of Diavolo's cousin, Turiddu, one whom the authorities had labelled a bandit but a man whom the peasantry regarded as a mixture of saint, protector, and provider. Here, in this very cave,' his glacial eyes raked the bare, stone-strewn floor, 'Maria's son was born. These walls were the first things he saw when he opened his eyes; this floor is the one upon which he crawled, this mountain was his playground. I know, because I am he!' Her start of surprise brought a nod of affirmation.

'Sì, signorina, I am Salvatore Diavolo, the only fish ever to escape your grandfather's net—and only because he is, as yet, unaware of my existence!'

Rosalba stared at the face that looked hewn out of the rock that had been his birthplace, her heart full of pity for the child who from birth had had to rely upon the protection of wild, lawless men in order to remain alive; it was hardly surprising that such a child should grow into a man steeped in resentment, having absorbed all the reckless defiance, the contempt of authority, the unruly passions of those who had served as his example. Seeds of hatred had been sown early so that now, in the fertility of manhood, they were blossoming, pushing forth strong roots that had to be fed on revenge in order to survive.

She shuddered, repelled by the fresh insight into her grandfather's nature and by the damage caused by Maria Pisciotta who had salvaged what remained of her pride by distorting the truth.

Spurred on by loyalty to her father, she defended

him gently: 'A woman in love, especially one whose love is not returned, often resorts to self-deception and allows pride to play tricks with conscience. My father was ignorant of the betrothal arranged between himself and your mother—there was no discussion, his opinion was never sought—in fact, when her name was mentioned as his future bride he had difficulty in recalling her to mind. He was a gentle-natured man, kind and always considerate of the feelings of others. You are wrong to assume that he inherited Conte Rossi's nature—they were completely opposed, even though they were father and son.'

'*Macchè!*' The derisive exclamation bounced off the walls and faded into the roof. 'The seed of the cedar will become cedar, the seed of the bramble can only become bramble!'

She sighed, knowing it was pointless to argue further. 'What do you intend doing with me?' she trembled.

'I intend,' he leant towards her to stress, 'that you will live as we have lived.'

'We ...?' she faltered, scared blue eyes roving their solitude.

'Myself, my parents, and the only family I ever knew—the band of brave men who were forced by men like your grandfather to take refuge in these caves, men branded criminals because they had the audacity to admit to ambitions, dreams and ideals. You will feel cold as my mother felt cold, suffer her discomforts, her loneliness, her fears. If the food is not to your liking you will go hungry, if your bed is too hard you will become stiff and weary with lack of sleep, but your most important function will be to act as bait to tempt the old snake out into the open so that his fangs may be drawn.'

'You intend to kill him?'

He paused, every muscle tense, his granite chin out-thrust. He communicated tension, a battle being fought within, so that when he slowly expelled a breath she unconsciously relaxed in unison. 'No,' he confessed, 'much as I would like to, I cannot. But there are others who can, and will. My task will be finished once I have handed him over to them.'

'How will he know where to come?' she said huskily, her throat tight.

'A message will be sent to him.'

'You can't do it!' she cried, clenching her fists into tight knots of desperation. 'You imply that you're incapable of killing in cold blood, yet if you deliver my grandfather into the hands of his enemies you'll be an accomplice—as much at fault as the man who actually plunges in the dagger! However hard you try to delude yourself that to carry out the practice of vendetta is an honourable obligation, the real truth is that you're indulging in hatred, in a lust for vengeance. No one is justified in taking the law into his own hands, such impunity would result in crime stalking the land, like a mad dog spreading its poison throughout the pack. To go back on society is to go back on life itself! Please try to forgive my grandfather—or, better still, forget him, because if you go through with this plan you will be morally guilty of his murder—of two murders,' she corrected, choking back tears, 'for if the vendetta is

to reach its customary conclusion your friends must
also kill me!'

Her unusual flow of eloquence petered into noth-
ingness, silenced by a look from hard, unrepentant
eyes that were roving, calculating, assessing her
trembling body.

His manner was aloof, his voice calm to the point
of laziness, when coolly he stated: 'Poor men with
nothing in their bellies welcome diversion even
more than they welcome food. The inhabitants of
these mountains are always hungry—their frugal
instincts would revolt against the thought of allowing the talents of a nubile young woman to be
wasted.'

CHAPTER SEVEN

It was desperately hot. Outside the cave was like an oven, inside was stifling and dense with flies. Ants as big as spiders crawled everywhere, lizards darted out of the shadows, the startling suddenness of their appearance causing Rosalba more repugnance even than their scaly, dragon-like bodies.

Diavolo had laughed unkindly at her horror of these creatures. He had left her alone after depositing the suitcase at her feet and ordering her to dress, but had returned hurriedly when at her first sight of a deep green lizard flickering up the cracked wall of the cave, its eyes brilliant and beady as they were caught by a ray of sunshine, she had screamed.

'They are harmless,' he had grinned. 'As a boy I spent many entertaining hours catching them. Watch, I will show you.' He had stepped outside and returned with a long stem of grass fashioned at one end into a running noose. 'You must creep up on them very slowly,' he had demonstrated. 'The lizard watches you, not the noose. You bring it gently, very gently, over his head ... like so ... he is mesmerised ... suddenly you pull the noose tight and *eccolo*!' To her disgust he had dangled the lizard, fluttering helplessly at the end of the grass fishing line, under her nose.

'You're cruel,' she had gasped, 'to inflict unnecessary pain upon creatures, however horrible!' She had cringed away when he had stroked a finger along the length of the lizard's scaly body.

'I do not agree that these small creatures are horrible, and you are mistaken in thinking that I killed it merely for sport. In these sparse mountain regions nothing is wasted, everything that is edible is eaten, everything that can serve a purpose is utilised. The lizard is a case in point; when dried and pounded up it will make very good medicine.'

Left once more alone, her skin crawling with disgust, her eyes searching warily for any approach of the reptiles she found so abhorrent, Rosalba snapped open the locks of her suitcase and lifted the lid. Her consternation as she began sorting through its contents was indescribable.

'Oh, Aprile,' she wailed, 'how on earth could you have expected me to wear these!'

The items in the suitcase were expressions of her cousin's impish humour and of her avowed intention to jerk Rosalba out of her sedate rut so that she might begin to embrace the sophisticated cult of her own generation. The outfits displayed at the fashion show had all been startling, but Aprile had chosen for her cousin the most daring, the most outrageous of them all.

One by one Rosalba unpacked them, her already low spirits growing more and more leaden as she searched for a suitable pair of slacks and discovered only pants of supple black leather made to fit tightly as a second skin or, at the other ridiculous extreme, gauzy culottes glitter-striped to resemble the pattern of a spider's web. She puzzled over strapless gowns, wondering about the powers of suspension, then concluding reluctantly that to wear such a gown would require placing great trust upon ruching elastic, whalebone or, failing these, sheer personal willpower.

Becoming more and more exasperated, she discarded strapless basques, boned and lace-trimmed; tops that were no more than tubes of material ruched to cling without any further means of support, and other totally unsuitable articles created out of glossy satin, imitating the clinging, vampish trend of the Twenties. She became a little less depressed when she discovered tucked into the side pocket of the suitcase a packet containing half a dozen pairs of filmy, shimmering briefs but, although she emptied the case entirely in order to be sure, there was no sign of a bra.

'Oh, glory ...!' she muttered, sitting back on her heels, insects and reptiles taking second place to the major catastrophe of being forced to titillate her abductor's sadistic humour by appearing before him dressed like a clown. An advancing line of giant ants spurred her into action. Grabbing a hasty selection of garments, she piled the remaining froth of satin and lace back into the suitcase and snapped shut the lid, then, stepping well out of line of the advancing army, she squeezed into black leather pants, pulled a tubular top over her head, then as protection from the sun, shrugged bare shoulders into a loose-fitting red satin jacket, heavily frilled around edges and wide-cuffed sleeves.

Her choice of footwear was limited, so without hesitation she discarded spindle-heeled evening shoes in favour of backless wooden clogs with tops of smooth soft leather that clung lovingly around her bare feet. She was ready! Drawing in a deep breath of apprehension, she stepped outside the cave and stood with eyes downcast, nerves braced for an attack of snarling humour.

He was lounging against a boulder smoking a cheroot, his eyes tracing the far horizon, much as his bandit friends must have done in the days when every moving speck upon the plain below was interpreted as a sign of danger. Rosalba heard a sharp intake of breath, and knew that he had become aware of her presence. When pebbles crunched beneath his heels she tensed, warned of his approach.

'Well, well!' As she had expected, the humour in his voice was not kind. Knowing that his mouth would be twisted into a derisive sneer, she refused to look up, even when he stripped the jacket from her shoulders and flung it with distaste across his shoulder. 'I did not spell out the need for serviceable clothing, *signorina*, because I gave you credit for having sufficient sense to choose wisely—instead of which you present yourself dressed as if for a masquerade! Are you really as naïve as you pretend, or have you perhaps decided to embark upon a scheme of seduction, setting out deliberately to tantalise, hoping the attraction of your body might have a softening effect upon my brain? That would be a very dangerous game to play with a man who is a wholly human, full blooded member of a notoriously virile race.'

'I had no choice ...' The threat behind his words provoked a stammered denial. 'The clothes in the suitcase aren't mine ... or at least,' honesty made her stumble, 'they are, but I had no hand in choosing them.'

'No?' The amusement in his voice was contradicted by eyes sparking steel. 'The clothes were packed in a suitcase bearing your initials, the suitcase had been delivered to your bedroom and placed beside your bed, yet you expect me to believe that they do not belong to you? Cheap women wear cheap clothes!' He jerked her forward into his arms. 'We Sicilians have a great affinity with the Arabs who greatly influenced our culture—which is probably why we subscribe to their theory that whatever can be seen can be touched!'

To her horror she felt his hands slip underneath the accommodating elasticated top and stiffened as his fingers began tracing a pathway of fire beneath her shoulderblades, under her arms, then closed to form firm, sinewed cups within which he enclosed each of her smooth breasts. Her shocked immobility could have been mistaken for either indifference or invitation. He opted for the latter. Suddenly his satanically cruel head swooped upon a mouth quivering with unutterable fear and from the moment their lips met a fire leapt to life somewhere deep within her, heating her blood into lava that coursed molten through her veins, consuming shame, protest, willpower—everything she attempted to throw in its path.

She made one feeble attempt to pull away, but was immediately reclaimed to suffer the hard thrust of his body that moulded against her own with an insistence that was terrifying yet hypnotic, repugnant yet at the same time compelling in an unbelievably shameless way. She could not respond because she did not know how. Tossed in a whirlpool of strange new emotions, she clung to his shirt-front as if to a lifeline and almost fell to her knees when, with an impatient curse, he pushed her away.

'The music is in you, *signorina*, but I am not to be permitted to play it, eh? Your desire matches mine, but you have a part to play, a wish to convince me that a Rossi need not be a she-devil, but can be cool, sweet, and gentle as a dove. So be it, *viso d'angelo*, continue with your charade!'

'I'm no angel,' she denied in an ashamed whisper, 'but you, *signore*, are an animal, a brute, a devil in nature as in name.'

She wanted to stamp her foot in anger when he threw back his head and laughed. Stooping to heave a loaded haversack on to his back, he took his time adjusting the shoulder-straps before quipping: 'And you, angel face, after spending days and nights alone in my company, will be considered by everyone who hears of it to be Diavolo's angel—the derogatory title bestowed by your grandfather upon my mother. You must forgive me for revelling in the anticipation of acquainting the Conte with the knowledge that his granddaughter's character has been destroyed by his own venom.'

Before abandoning the cave where the jeep was still garaged he rolled a huge stone in front of the entrance, then camouflaged the remaining gap with brushwood, more of which he used to sweep the dusty plateau free of indented tyre treads. When he was satisfied that no tell-tale marks remained he ordered her to walk around the stony perimeter where no footprints could be traced, then began urging her upwards along a path climbing almost perpendicular to the top of the mountain.

'You expect me to climb in these?' she protested, extending a clog-shod foot.

'I do not expect, I demand that you do so,' he crisped. 'When the going gets hard I shall give you a hand.'

Dubiously, she eyed him. With a loaded haversack on his back and her suitcase in one hand it did not seem likely that much help would be forthcoming. Yet the dread of what might happen if she refused to obey made her grit her teeth and follow in his wake.

She had had the presence of mind to retrieve the jacket he had taken such a dislike to, and was glad of its protection as the sun beamed upon her back, causing her to sweat profusely. In no time at all her hair was a mass of damp tendrils—a clinging silver cap—her jacket a mass of dark stains, and the skin-tight pants she had considered comparatively serviceable were reduced to the basis of drainpipes channelling rivulets of sweat down her legs. Grimly, she hung on to her clogs, preferring to slither and slide on loose stones rather than risk having the soles of her feet flint-ripped and embedded with grit.

He glanced back only occasionally, and for these moments she reserved a composed expression which she switched on immediately she saw his head beginning to turn. Her discomfort afforded him pleasure; a stubbornness she had not known she possessed goaded her into ensuring that he gained as little satisfaction as possible from her agony.

A long, painful hour passed before he called a halt. Sitting down on a large flat boulder, he beckoned her to join him, then eased the haversack from his shoulders and began rummaging inside in search of a flask.

'A drink will not come amiss,' he suggested, unscrewing the top before he handed it over.

Eagerly she grabbed it, put the neck of the flask to her lips, and tipped back her head. Nothing she had previously drunk tasted half so delicious as the lukewarm water that trickled over her tongue, then sidled blissfully down her parched throat. 'Thank you,' she gasped, handing back the flask after downing half its contents, 'I was dying of thirst!'

He took a casual swig, then replaced the cap. 'You are a poor, useless creature,' he stated with contempt. 'Muscles are meant to be used, bodies meant to be kept at the peak of physical perfection, yet among city people there is a preponderance of flab. Up yonder,' he nodded towards the peak above them, 'live women who think nothing of travelling this path five or six times a day to tend crops growing on the lower slopes, women twice your age who have known not a fraction of the luxuries you take so much for granted.'

She edged away until she had put a foot of space between them. His close proximity had re-aroused the strange, powerful yearnings she could not fathom but which she knew were wanton and wicked. Panicking lest his sharp, intuitive mind should probe her secret, she conquered tongue-tying shyness sufficiently to stammer:

VISIT 4 MAGIC PLACES FREE!

AFRICA

Time of the Temptress by Violet Winspear
Trapped in the jungles of Africa, Eve's only chance for survival was total dependence on the mercenary Major Wade O'Mara. He had the power to decide her fate. But only she could make him give in to desire.

GREECE

Say Hello to Yesterday by Sally Wentworth
Seeing Nick after seven years made Holly realize it was her parents who ruined their marriage. Now that she had found him, she knew that their love had never died. And she was determined to make him love her again.

CARIBBEAN

Born Out of Love by Anne Mather
Charlotte had paid for one night's pleasure with years of pain and loneliness. Ten years after Logan had deserted her and the baby, they met unexpectedly on San Cristobal... where their love affair seemed destined to begin again.

ENGLAND

Man's World by Charlotte Lamb
She had everything going for her. Brains. Beauty. And a sterling wit. Her only problem was men. She hated them. That is, until Eliot decided to make her see otherwise.

Love surrounds you in the pages of Harlequin Romances

Harlequin Presents romance novels are the ultimate in romantic fiction...the kind of stories that you can't put down...that take you to romantic places in search of adventure and intrigue. They are stories full of the emotions of love...full of the hidden turmoil beneath even the most innocent-seeming relationships. Desperate clinging love, emotional conflict, bold lovers, destructive jealousies and romantic imprisonment—you'll find it all in the passionate pages of **Harlequin Presents** romance novels.

Let your imagination roam to the far ends of the earth. Meet true-to-life people. Become intimate with those who live larger than life.

Harlequin Presents romance novels are the kind of books you just can't put down...the kind of experiences that remain in your dreams long after you've read about them.

Let your imagination roam to romantic places when you...

BUSINESS REPLY CARD

First Class   Permit No. 70   Tempe, AZ

POSTAGE WILL BE PAID BY ADDRESSEE

Harlequin Reader Service
1440 South Priest Drive
Tempe, Arizona 85266

NO POSTAGE
NECESSARY
IF MAILED
IN THE
UNITED STATES

'People actually live up there?'

'Yes. An entire village,' he replied sourly. 'And before you ask the usual inane question, why, let me assure you that people born and bred in the mountains prefer isolation to so-called civilisation and that far from envying the life style of their more comfortably-off brothers, they actually enjoy their hard daily grind.'

'Will we be staying in the village?' she ventured timidly.

'No, we will not.' Forcibly he rammed the flask back into the haversack. 'The village inhabitants have suffered enough retribution in the past through harbouring outlaws; I do not intend to allow your grandfather's wrath to fall once more upon the heads of my friends.'

'Then where ...?'

'You'll find out soon enough,' he told her brusquely. 'Come, sitting here we are as visible as flies upon a wall. By this time your grandfather will have been notified of your absence, and also of the reason why. Search parties will have been organised—we must be out of sight before they reach here.'

They stopped once more at midday for a lunch of bread and cheese. There was no conversation, for she was too exhausted to speak and reserved what strength she had left for the last haul up to the summit which by this time was looming almost overhead. Her feet were sore and blistered, the inside of her legs chafed by leather seams. She longed to collapse on to the arid, dusty ground and sob out all her pent-up misery, yet pride stiffened her slight body erect and the tears pressing at the back of dark violet eyes were not allowed to fall.

'*You will suffer as my mother suffered,*' he had promised. Obviously he was a man of his word.

The worst heat of the sun was fading by the time they reached their goal. It was bliss to stagger inside a large cave where, regardless of ants, lizards, and powdery dust, she sank to her knees unashamedly, panting as she fought to recover from the most gruelling physical exertion she had ever experienced.

He ignored her plight, stepping past her to grunt satisfaction at the sight of a pile of provisions stacked in a corner of the cave. When he disappeared into the murky background she heard the echo of his retreating footsteps and guessed that the cave was an ante-chamber linked to a second chamber by a tunnel. During their ascent she had noted the existence of many caves and realised that the mountain was honeycombed with them, most of them probably connecting, and that any person familiar with their geography could retreat inside the mountain at the first hint of danger, reappear and disappear at will, to mock baffled pursuers.

He was gone for ages and by the time he returned she was shivering in damp clothes that had turned more and more clammy as the temperature both inside and outside the cave began to drop.

'I'll build a fire.' She was sitting nursing her knees when his voice speared out of the darkness behind her.

'Is that safe?' she questioned, her eyes anxious. 'Won't the smoke be seen?' It was only when the words had been uttered that she realised how ridiculous they must have sounded in the circumstances.

He, too, was quick to realise her blunder, yet there was slightly less jeer in his tone, and more than a hint of surprise when he congratulated: 'You really are the most accommodating person to kidnap, *signorina*—one might almost suspect that you do not wish to be freed from captivity!'

'Of course I want to return home,' she contradicted, blushing hotly in the darkness, 'but I wasn't thinking of myself.'

'You are worried on my account ...?' His eyebrows winged.

'Certainly not ...' Her tongue seemed stuck to the roof of her mouth. 'I abhor violence,' she managed to stammer. 'You've admitted that you intend to manoeuvre my grandfather out into the open so that your pack of bloodthirsty friends can pounce upon him. But things could go wrong and it could be yourself who is killed. Isn't there any other way?' she urged desperately. 'Couldn't you both agree to a compromise?'

'*Compromise!*' He spat the word into the dust. 'You ask me to seek appeasement with a man who has wiped out every male member of my family? No, I will not compromise— nor will I ever withdraw my support from the fight against wrong. Naturally, I would like peace of mind, I have no wish to spend the rest of my life tormented by thoughts of revenge, which is why this vendetta must be concluded. Peace will begin for me the moment your grandfather's reign of terror is brought to an end.'

Food, well wrapped up to protect it from marauding ants, had been left in the cave, together with sleeping bags, soap, towels and sufficient kindling to start a fire. Later that evening, she relaxed in the warmth of the fire, nibbling a chicken joint, watching the play of fireglow and shadows over his dark features. He was sitting opposite, entirely absorbed in demolishing his share of supper, and when finally he was satisfied that his chicken bone had been gnawed clean, he threw it into the fire, then looked up suddenly and caught her watching him.

Confusion swept over her, yet her eyes were held by an expression on his face that she could not fathom—an expression visible for only a fraction of a second before it was wiped clean and cynicism took over. Had she imagined that for an infinitesimal space of time his eyes had softened as they met hers, that his grim line of mouth had quirked into a half-smile of companionship, of shared enjoyment?

His harsh question dispelled this illusion. 'How old are you, *signorina*? I ask, because at this moment, with tendrils of hair curling round your face and eyes heavy with the approach of sleep, you appear to be little more than a child.'

'I'm twenty-two years old!' she protested, furthering his impression of naïveté by emulating the indignation of an adolescent aspiring to maturity.

'Confucius said,' he grinned, 'that there are cases when the blade springs but the plant does not go on to flower. There are cases where it flowers but no fruit is subsequently produced. You puzzle me,' he admitted, growing grave, 'I cannot decide whether you are a tight little plant whose bud has not yet broken into flower, or whether you have been many times pollinated and are subsequently fruitful.'

His almost lazy questioning of her virginity sent a rush of colour to her cheeks. She was grateful that the fireglow disguised her shame, leaving him no clue to the mortification she was feeling as he continued, so casually he might have been thinking aloud:

'Young Englishwomen, I've been told, are dedicated to the premise that variety is the spice of love. I suppose, therefore, that it is a natural follow-up for such liberated ladies to consider themselves experts in sexual skills. Yet, for me, such a partner would hold little appeal. When two people make love they are sharing the most personal as well as the most beautiful of all human experiences, which is why, when I take a wife, I shall expect her to look to me for guidance. Have you discovered,' he suddenly leant forward to address her frozen stillness, 'that the more experienced a woman becomes the more difficulty she has in finding an adequate partner?' Mercifully, he did not wait for an answer. 'Yes,' he nodded, regarding her from under hooded lids, 'this, I think, is the area in which Englishmen are most likely to suffer—and their womenfolk too—for all of your sex, whatever they might profess to the contrary, want to be dominated. Confess, *signorina*!' he hissed across the width of the fire, startling her out of her wits, 'confess that your basic, intrinsic need is to be grabbed by the hair and dragged into bed!'

Rosalba stared at features made to look incredibly satanic by the reflection of fire flickering in the deep pits of his eyes, by shadows that darkened the hollows beneath his cheekbones and lengthened the lean profile that narrowed gradually to a belligerent chin. His teeth showed white as he smiled, a smile so humourless she shuddered, so devilish she would not have been in the least surprised to have seen horns sprouting from his head.

The atmosphere felt inflammable, as if one spirited word would be enough to trigger off an explosion. She was petrified, too completely out of her depth to formulate any reply. Aprile would have enjoyed the challenge, would have found no difficulty in choosing some appropriate quip, but so far as this subject was concerned Rosalba's mind was a sheet of virgin paper, spotless and entirely blank.

As his eyes remained fastened upon her face she would have been astonished to learn how cool and composed she appeared, how serene her expression, how steady the eyes that met his. When finally, after one last sardonic glint, he broke his mesmerising hold, she almost sagged with relief.

'Time for sleep, *signorina*.' He sounded disgruntled, his voice edged with frustration.

'Good ... goodnight, *signore*.' She backed slowly towards her sleeping bag, then, as she climbed into it, stuttered the ultimate banality: 'P-pleasant dreams ...'

CHAPTER EIGHT

Rosalba dozed fitfully, opening her eyes at the slightest sound, at the slightest movement of the figure who had taken up his position at the mouth of the cave as soon as she had retired to her sleeping bag, and had remained there, alert and watchful, ever since.

'A pack of wild dogs has been reported roaming the hillsides. Also foxes are an ever-present danger,' he had told her, obliquely explaining the rifle laid across his knee.

He was a strange man, she pondered drowsily, a mass of contradictions—one minute cold as ice, the next fiery as Etna, the volcano that dominated the island. It was as if he were not quite at ease playing the role that had been thrust upon him, as if there were two separate personalities warring within him with the result that at times he was not quite as ruthless as he threatened to be, nor yet as tender and thoughtful as she had begun to suspect he could be.

Her reverie was broken at the sight of a shadowy outline that had appeared out of the darkness and was bending to whisper into Salvatore's ear. She heard quick, garbled words that she could not understand, with frequent reference and much stress placed upon the words *il dottore*, from which she concluded that someone was in urgent need of medical assistance. When both shadows moved inside the cave she saw illuminated by the dying embers of the fire the face of a boy, his brow puckered with worry as once more he emitted a spate of words that sounded very much like an entreaty.

Salvatore nodded, then patted the boy on the shoulder before striding across the cave to bend across her sleeping bag. 'Are you awake?'

'Yes.' She struggled upright.

'Get dressed, we must go down into the village.'

'What, at this time of night?'

'Yes,' he affirmed irritably. 'How long will it take you to get dressed?'

'I haven't undressed,' she surprised him by saying.

'Oh, good ... Then come with me and make as little noise as possible. Your grandfather has set many men on our trail, it is imperative that we avoid hasty encounters during which an impulsive finger might activate a trigger. I want your soft white neck to remain intact, at least until my ransom demands have been met.'

So he wanted money as well as vengeance! Her heart ached with disillusionment as she stumbled in his wake through dark passages linking cave with cave, sometimes rising, sometimes descending, but always rough underfoot and harbouring—she had no shadow of a doubt—hundreds of loathsome, four-legged creatures. Her feet were raw by the time they emerged into the open and she became aware, just visible in the dusk of the valley below, of a huddle of houses sliced through by one main road leading straight to the door of the inevitable church complete with bell tower and steeple.

All the houses were in darkness with the exception of one from which intermittent light was beaming through a window. Once, twice, three times the light flashed, then came a pause before the light began flashing again. Salvatore spoke to the boy, who nodded and ran off into the shadows. Five minutes later a bird call pierced the air.

'All's well!' He gripped her by the elbow. 'It is now safe for us to go down.'

'Why ...?' Rosalba began, curiosity all-consuming.

'I'll explain later,' he silenced her sharply. 'Just keep quiet and follow me.'

She obeyed without argument, hopping and squirming behind him in an effort to ease the now agonising pain of feet blistered from toe to heel. When a piece of grit became lodged between her foot and the sole of her shoe she only just managed to suppress a scream and though she fought her weakness tears were streaming down her cheeks by the time they reached their destination—a small house in a mean, narrow street, its door and windows shuttered.

Salvatore knocked softly, three times, then after a short wait the inner door opened and Rosalba saw a pair of eyes peering through the shutters, which were then opened just far enough to allow them to squeeze through before they were re-closed, together with the interior door which was banged shut and locked immediately they stepped inside a small living-room. As they moved towards a perimeter of light being cast by a lamp suspended from the ceiling, a thin quavering voice came from the direction of a bed that looked as if it had been squeezed into a too-tight corner. Its frail occupant showed no sign of discomfort, however, as she adored Salvatore with her eyes, yet both joy and censure were evident in her tone.

'Toto! They had no right to send for you, I begged them not to. You must go! Think of the risk you run!'

'*Ridicolo,* Zia Giuseppina, you know I would have been very angry indeed if they had not informed me of your illness. Now,' he sat down on the edge of the bed and encircled her wrist with lean brown fingers, 'describe to me exactly how you are feeling.'

The old lady whom he had addressed as aunt tried to make light of her ailment, yet her wrinkled face, deeply scored with lines of pain, made her suffering self-evident. Rosalba was amazed at the professional ease with which Salvatore probed and questioned, the way his fingers gently searched and seemed to pinpoint exactly the source of pain. When finally he replaced the bedcovers and tucked the ends under the old lady's chin he was frowning, yet he sounded deliberately light as he assured her:

'A few days' rest and cosseting is all that you need, Zia. I want you to take this medicine and in the morning I'll make arrangements for someone to attend to your needs. Meanwhile, try to sleep and rest easy, I shall be near at hand if you should need me.'

She gave in without argument, and after downing the medicine nestled back against her pillows, her face aglow with a smile of contentment. Salvatore remained by the bedside until her light breathing developed a heavier, stertorous tone, then, his expression grim, he moved away to eye Rosalba who was slumped wearily on a hard wooden chair.

'I'm pleased that you have managed to make yourself comfortable. No, stay where you are,' he directed when she began struggling upright. 'Zia Giuseppina cannot be left, we must remain here until morning.'

'What's wrong with her?' She rubbed sleep from her eyes and tried to look alert.

'She has a chronic ailment,' he clamped. 'An operation at its onset would have saved her many years of agony.'

'Then why didn't she have one?' She flinched from his look of hard dislike, a look that seemed to indicate that he held her in some way responsible for the old lady's plight.

'Because there was no one available to diagnose the illness, because there was no one who cared sufficiently about the health and welfare of those who live in the mountain regions, and also, as was once pointed out to me in the dry, philosophical way that is so characteristic of my people, there is little enough money to spare for the living, so it does not make sense to waste any on one who might be dying.' When she reacted with a shocked start he derided: 'Ah, yes, you have a right to look appalled, *signorina*! In your country, it is law that a percentage of earnings and profits has to be set aside to provide free medical attention for all who need it, but here in my country there is a man who feels entitled to channel the profits from sweated labour towards the purchase of yet another fountain intended to glorify the name of a dynasty that has become synonymous with cruelty, selfishness and greed. But enough of futile talk!' She felt crushed as the ant that fell foul of his grinding heel. 'I must leave you here alone for a while—do not be foolish enough to try to escape unless you wish to find yourself alone in the mountains at the mercy of foxes and ravenous wild dogs.'

Rosalba shuddered and pulled her chair closer to the bed; even in sleep, the old lady's presence was comforting—there were times when her abductor's barely controlled savagery made her wonder if she would not be safer at the mercy of wild animals whose threat was merely physical rather than to have to endure the mental torture inflicted by the lash of his contemptuous tongue.

The room was comfortably warm and soon her head began to nod. She slipped sideways in her chair until her head and arm found a vacant resting space at the foot of the bed. A couple of hours must have passed when the feeble stirring of a foot jerked her awake.

'How are you feeling now?' she enquired gently as the old lady's bird-bright eyes raked her face.

'Better,' she replied, unsmiling. 'Where is Toto?'

'Toto?' Suddenly realising that this was probably a family contraction of Salvatore, Rosalba assured her hastily: 'He is not far away, shall I try to find him for you?'

'No, no . . .' a feeble arm waved dissent. 'I'm quite comfortable, I merely wish to be certain that he is safe.'

'Perhaps he has gone to fetch a doctor,' Rosalba suggested hopefully.

'A doctor?' The old lady's stare was incredulous. 'But Toto *is* a doctor, didn't you know? The finest, cleverest doctor in all the world!'

It was Rosalba's turn to stare. For a second she did not assimilate the meaning of the old lady's words and when eventually she did a laughing denial gurgled, then died in her throat as she recalled small puzzling incidents that now fell into place forming a feasible pattern: the boy's frequent use of the word *dottore* when he had rushed into the cave with his garbled message; the expert way in which the old lady had been examined; the knowledgeable questions that had been put to her; the slim, brown, yet well-kept hands that had searched for a pulse and most of all, she realised with a flash of insight, his puzzling reluctance to be the one to physically conclude the vendetta that had raged for years between her family and his. Normally, as the last of a long line of men who had perished at her grandfather's command, he would be expected to relish the ultimate act of revenge, but a doctor was dedicated to the saving of life so, however much tempted he was, it would go greatly against his code of ethics to kill!

'You have heard of Turiddu?' The old lady seemed eager to talk so, hoping it might help her to forget her pain, Rosalba did not discourage her. 'He was my son!' The old face beamed with pride. 'Not a bandit, as some would have you think,' she hissed fiercely, 'but a *bravo ragazzo, molto sincero, molto religioso, gentilissimo* and *molto bello* with beautiful eyes and smile that set the heart of every girl a-flutter. His only faults were a hatred of in-justice and a strong admiration for anything he con-sidered noble or generous. He was my youngest and most beautiful child,' she quavered. 'Whenever I see Toto I am reminded of him, for in both looks and ways he is more akin to my son than to his own father.'

Something about Rosalba's fervent nod of agree-ment made the old lady suspicious of her allegiance. 'Who are you?' she asked sharply. 'You must know Toto well or he would not have brought you here.'

Not daring to mention the hated name of Rossi, Rosalba prevaricated: 'We are ... friends,' she stumbled over the description.

But the old lady looked satisfied. 'Good, then Toto will have told you about my son, how, for the sake of a petty crime, a crime hundreds of others were committing at the time, he was condemned to being hunted like an animal for the rest of his young life.' In a dreamy tone she began reliving the past, her work-ravaged hands resting relaxed and still on top of the ancient blanket.

'After the war, food became very scarce when the Allies arrived, particularly the Americans who were all very rich and could afford to pay whatever price was asked for the small amount of goods that were available. Prices rose well above our means, but even if we could have afforded it, grain was un-available because unscrupulous men were hoarding supplies for sale on the black market. A law was passed, making it illegal to transport foodstuff from one province to another, Carabinieri patrolled pro-vince boundaries and searched everyone who passed for contraband. But those who had money to spare greased their palms so that the Carabinieri turned a blind eye, therefore only the poor who could not afford the bribes were caught.

'My son, Turiddu, could not stand to see the children of our village starving, so he and his elder brother coaxed a friendly farmer to let them have two sacks of grain which they carried on their backs —they had no mule—miles across country. They were caught,' she sighed deeply, 'and although they had between them a small sum of money my sons were too proud to bribe the soldiers. Their identity cards were demanded, the two sacks of grain confiscated, and both of my boys threatened with the *bastinado* if they did not reveal from whom they had bought the grain. The *bastinado*, you understand, meant a beating on the feet with rifle butts. Naturally, they refused to betray their friend, and as they were pleading with the soldiers, explaining the circumstances existing in our village, a man appeared all unsuspecting leading a grain-laden mule. When the soldiers pounced on him my sons were left being guarded by only one man with a machine-gun. Bravely,' she trembled, 'Turiddu attacked the guard, crashing his elbow against the barrel of the gun and knocking it from his hands. As they ran for cover into the bamboos the soldiers opened fire behind them and they were wounded, yet they managed to reach the safety of the mountain which was to become their permanent hideout. Turiddu was just a boy,' she pleaded for Rosalba's understanding, 'a wild, reckless boy whose loyalty and sympathy was outraged by the treatment received by his people, yet basically he was gentle and kind. Toto's father knew that, which is why he did not hesitate to place his wife and their unborn child under his cousin's protection.'

Moved almost to tears by the simply-told tale, Rosalba choked out a question, subconsciously seeking corroboration of the Diavolo family's thirst for vengeance. 'They were fleeing from someone who wished them harm?' she asked tentatively.

The old lady did not hesitate. 'From Conte Rossi,' she affirmed with such lack of heat Rosalba was forced to believe her.

'Something has always puzzled me,' Rosalba did not want to overtax the old lady's strength, but as this was probably to be her one and only chance of finding out the truth, she probed, 'why did a proud, aristocratic man like the Conte wish his son to marry a girl who was, after all, just a peasant? Surely the daughter of some other aristocratic family would have been a more characteristic choice?'

Her reply was a humourless cackle. 'The cunning old snake was disenchanted with women of his own class. His own wife, after giving him but two children, was rendered barren—we mountain women, though poorly brought up, have strong, healthy bodies. Fourteen children in one family is not unusual for us.'

'You mean the Conte selected Maria as a wife for his son simply because of her ability to supply him with heirs?'

'Why else ...?' The old lady sounded suddenly weary. 'Yet Maria was so besotted with the idea of one day becoming a *contessa* she would not believe

it—if she had,' her voice dropped to a regretful sigh,
'we might not today be placing so many wreaths
upon so many graves.'

'So you admit that Maria herself was not entirely
blameless?' Rosalba urged, and was answered by a
stern voice from the doorway. She did not know how
much he had overheard, but Salvatore was angry, of
that there was no doubt.

'Have you so little conscience that you think nothing of disturbing an ailing woman from her sleep?'
His body was fluid, animal-fierce, as he stalked
towards the bed.

'The fault was mine, Toto.' The old lady's eyes
begged forgiveness. 'Your young friend has been
very sweet, very thoughtful, and tolerant of an old
woman's ramblings. I was glad of her company, for I
cannot sleep.'

'Then I must make you,' he scolded, reaching
into his haversack to withdraw a large tin that rat-
tled when he unscrewed the top. It was almost three-
quarters full of pills, two of which he shook into the
palm of his hand. He poured a glass of water from
a pitcher at the bedside, then, showing no trace of
his former irritation, he slid an arm around her
shoulders and propped her upright as he instructed:
'Here, swallow these.'

Rosalba's heart leapt as a daring idea presented
itself. Carefully she noted every detail of the box
of pills that had suddenly presented itself as a means
of escape to freedom. She had no hope of opposing
his superior strength, but if she could manage to
filch some of the sleeping pills, if she chose carefully
the time and the place, she might stand a very good

chance of escape from the man whose excuse for her abduction was a proud desire for vengeance, but who seemingly, by his own admission, was not averse to lining his pockets with her grandfather's money.

She shied from examining the question of why the fact that her kidnapper—a man well qualified to step into the shoes of a notorious bandit—had been proved mercenary should hurt so much. Or why, as his dark head bent to place a light kiss upon a withered cheek, she should experience a stab of emotion almost akin to envy ...

CHAPTER NINE

'KEEP still,' her captor ordered absently when Rosalba tried to squirm out of his reach. He was bathing her feet, a daily torture—unknown to him —of delicious shivering and a hot shrinking from his touch, that had begun the morning after he had been called to his aunt's bedside when she had stood up, then fallen back into her chair with a sharp cry of pain brought about by blisters so painful they could no longer be ignored.

His lips had tightened into a line of annoyance when, brushing aside her attempt to make light of her pain, he had insisted upon examining her feet. As she had submitted to his tender probing her shy eyes had dared to linger upon his downbent head, admiring the blue-black density of hair springing strongly from his scalp, twisting and whirling as if each strand had individual life, tracing a profile etched cameo-sharp, lingering upon thick lashes smudging black crescents against his cheeks. Then, as her eyes had slid downward, she had looked quickly away, bracing herself to combat the anger demonstrated by a fiercely out-thrust jaw. But the anger had not fallen upon her head. Instead, he had almost apologised for his thoughtlessness when, in a curiously strangled voice, he had muttered:

'The feet of mountain people are so tough shoes could be dispensed with altogether—and often are.'

That had occurred almost a week ago and every day since he had bathed and dusted them with antiseptic powder until now they were almost as good as new.

He said as much, easing up from his knees with a grunt of satisfaction. 'You should be feeling quite comfortable now.'

'I am,' she assured him with such gratitude he winced.

'Most girls,' he admitted dryly, gathering up the medicaments he had used, 'would not hesitate to point out that it was my lack of foresight that caused the injury in the first place.

They were sitting just inside the cave, near enough to the entrance to enjoy the warmth of a dying sun yet far enough back to avoid being seen by searchers known to be scouring the plains below. Rosalba caught her breath in astonishment at the near-compliment. Salvatore looked up, his quick ears alerted by the sound, and as his piercing glance collided with soft eyes, dusk-darkened to violet, it seemed to Rosalba that at that very moment life was caught in an unending pause. Danger threatened all around, down in the valley men were searching the groves of huge, ancient olive trees, the orchards of peach and fig trees, the vineyards; combing mountains, disrupting the even tenor of life in every hamlet and village containing inhabitants suspected of allegiance to Diavolo. Yet during those magical seconds, as the sun sank below the horizon, as shadow replaced colour on the landscape and fireflies began dancing in the darkness, she forgot completely her reason for being there as she grappled with a new sensation that defied analysis or description, a conviction that here in the bosom of a purple mountain, with dusk for a cloak and the throbbing song of a nightingale for a lullaby, she had cast off her old existence and been born anew.

They emerged from their trance simultaneously, she breathless and shaken, he sounding terse with resentment.

'Time to visit Zia Giuseppina,' he clamped, snapping the delicate thread of intimacy by turning sharply away.

Jerked back to sanity, Rosalba struggled to master a humiliating suspicion that she had embarrassed him and tried to sound cool as she enquired:

'How was it possible for an orphan boy brought up in poverty to achieve professional status? You said yourself that money has always been scarce, and yet medical training is expensive.'

Far from resenting her prying questions, he seemed glad to take up the subject. 'I was fortunate enough to have relatives in America. My father's elder brother was accepted as an immigrant years before the war. He became a successful business man, rich by anyone's standards, so when I was ten years old he sent for me. I remained in America until my education was completed. When I had all the degrees I needed I returned home.'

His last three words betrayed more than he intended. 'You didn't like America?'

He hesitated. 'It is the ambition of every Sicilian peasant to emigrate there,' he told her slowly, 'a land of riches, friendship, equality and justice ...'

'And yet ...?' she prompted.

'And yet,' he swung round to send her a heart-stopping smile, 'what little spare time I had was spent in the zoo. There, among creatures of the wild, segregated into boxes, curbed by iron bars, their freedom restricted by boundaries enclosing them within the few short yards of territory they could be allowed, I felt a strong affinity.'

As, under the cover of darkness, they set off for the village, Rosalba stumbling in his wake, her heart ached with sympathy for a wild boy of the mountains who, at an unruly age, had been trapped, crated and labelled, then despatched to an alien land to suffer confinement within a succession of brick walls until he was suitably tamed, tutored, and finally stamped with the mark of civilisation's approval. What torture he must have endured! How many heartbroken sobs he must have stifled as night after night he rested his head on a pillow that was not stuffed with fragrant herbs, and stirred restlessly beneath a blanket that was not hand-woven nor even hand-spun with wool combed from the backs of animals roaming wild around his beloved hills and mountains.

Zia Giuseppina seemed greatly improved. As soon as they entered her room she jerked upright, quivering with an indignation that shook the bed.

'Toto, I *insist* that you give me permission to get out of bed, and also that you inform that idiot, Gina, whom you so foolishly elected my jailor, that I am perfectly fit and that she is to fetch me my clothes!'

His lips twitched, but he did not reply until he

had checked her pulse and concluded a swift examination.

'Very well, Zia,' he surrendered graciously. 'I am not entirely satisfied that you are as fit as you say you are, but if you promise to rest in your chair and to return to bed the moment you feel fatigued I will tell Gina to help you dress.'

His aunt's withered-olive face grew stubborn, her small dark eyes snapped mutiny, then with a shrug she gave in. 'Very well, Toto, you have my promise. But I still think,' she snapped, determined to have the last word, 'that you are being *ridicolo*. Much more of this treatment and my neighbours will think me senile. I do not wish to be pampered!'

'*Sì*, I understand,' he accepted the rebuke with gravity. 'You are *tenace*; remind me, if ever again I am tempted to forget.'

She scowled, suspecting irony, then her face broke into a smile as she extended her thin arms to envelop him in a warm hug. 'You are a good boy, Toto, even if at times you are a little too bold. Still, only the bold win the fair,' her sly glance slid towards Rosalba who was hovering in the background, 'as your young friend will no doubt agree.'

'My young *friend* ...!' A hot tide of colour engulfed Rosalba when she heard the incredulous stress he placed upon the word. 'But surely, Zia, you know who——' He stopped, suddenly thoughtful, then with a shrug concluded dryly: 'Time enough to shelter when the wind begins to blow.' He picked up his haversack. 'We must be on our way. Do not worry, Zia, if I do not visit you during the next few days, I'm expecting to be very busy.'

'Before you go,' she stopped him in his tracks, 'I have a small present for your friend. If you will wait outside, Toto,' she glanced pointedly towards the door, 'I should like to give it to her in private.'

He seemed about to argue, then changed his mind, swung his haversack upon his shoulder and strode towards the door. 'As you wish, but be as quick as you can,' he addressed Rosalba, 'and do not allow my aunt to exhaust herself, for she talks as she plays the harp, unceasingly, drowning in the music of her own words.'

But Zia Giuseppina was too pleased with herself to be indignant. After shooing him outside, she instructed in a voice trembling with anticipation: 'Go to that chest, my dear, pull out the middle drawer and fetch me the parcel you will find inside.'

Rosalba did as she was told, puzzled by the old lady's excitement and curious about the contents of the bundle she lifted out of the drawer, a soft, shapeless mound wrapped in a silken shawl.

'I want you to have these,' Zia Giuseppina's fingers trembled as she untied the single knot. 'They have been in my possession since I was a girl, but as I have no daughters and have no further use for them myself it would please me greatly if you would wear them.'

Rosalba gasped when the knot gave way and a froth of lace and yellow pleated cotton spilled out over the bed.

'Try them on,' Zia pleaded eagerly. 'Let me see how they look.'

Nothing loath, Rosalba scrambled out of the black leather pants she had begun to detest and into

a full-length skirt flounced from waist to hem with
alternate tiers of crisp saffron yellow cotton, pleated
like a fan, and beautiful hand-made lace. Next she
donned a white cotton shift with full sleeves caught
tight at the wrists and a drawstring neckline. Over
this she slipped a black velvet corset, low-boned to
accommodate breasts thrusting against the shift
when the corset was tightly laced up the front. But
the most gorgeous item of all was a lace-edged
apron that clung lovingly around her tiny waist, its
pristine background splashed with exquisitely embroidered poppies, their petals flame-red, flam-
boyant as courage, their hearts black as the devil
himself. She tied a small matching kerchief at the
back of her head, then poised expectantly, awaiting
the old lady's comments.

'*Bella innocenza! Bellezza rara!* Our national costume has never looked so well. Go, *signorina*, ask
Toto if he does not agree that his little friend is now
the most beautiful girl in the whole of Sicily!'

Stooping to press a kiss of pure affection upon the
old lady's cheek, Rosalba whirled from the room and
ran outside to search for him in the darkness.

Confident in the knowledge that their hunters
had been reported to have moved farther afield, she
flung joyfully through the doorway and cannoned
straight into him as he waited with his back turned
towards her, staring intently, his attention caught
by light spilling out of the windows of a building
and by a torrent of music, singing and shouts of
animated laughter pouring from its open door.

'What's going on?' she whispered. 'A wedding, a
family celebration ...?'

'Tomorrow is a day of fasting and abstinence,' he replied without turning his head, 'so tonight they feast, filling their bellies in readiness for a day of hunger.'

'And as they feast they dance, and as they dance they sing,' she concluded. 'It sounds great fun.'

They had by this time almost reached the entrance to the building that stood a little apart from the rest. It was bursting with people, resounding with a noise that was almost deafening. As they drew parallel, a man appeared on the threshold and stood blinking, adjusting his eyesight from brilliant light to sudden darkness. As he peered into their faces his vision cleared, and with a great shout of delight he grabbed Salvatore by the arm.

'Toto, my friend, come in, come and join us! You will be quite safe, the Conte's pack of wolves is long gone, but even so, we still have look-outs posted at strategic points. So you can relax for once, my friend, enjoy yourself, just for tonight forget your worries and remember only that you are among friends!'

The man's shout of welcome brought others pouring out of the building and in no time at all Salvatore was surrounded by a crowd of vociferous, back-slapping men who edged him inside, giving him no time to argue, no chance to catch so much as a glimpse of her finery.

She stood back dejected, watching his dark head disappearing out of sight, then reacted with a shock of fear when a harsh voice spoke behind her, instructing coldly:

'You, too, may go inside, Signorina *Rossi*!' He

spat her name. 'You will sit in a corner where you can be watched while you await Diavolo's pleasure.'

Inside the building that consisted of just one large room, its bare walls festooned with ribbons and garlands of flowers, wooden forms were tiered around three of the walls, leaving space in the middle of the floor for the many couples who were dancing. Although she was squeezed into a corner and then left, Rosalba could not feel isolated with dozens of hostile eyes trained upon her face. She was one of the hated Rossis. She shivered, feeling for the first time in her life ashamed of a name which previously had always seemed to ring proud.

When she dared to look around she saw that the rest of the women were also wearing national costume, many with an additional gold-embroidered veil falling down to their shoulders. Salvatore was lost in the wild mêlée, she caught occasional glimpses of his lithe figure as he joined in the fun, whirling past with a different girl for each of the intricate folk dances.

Gradually, as she became less conscious of the hostility being projected, she was able to relax and observe examples of ancient Sicilian protocol as men approached prospective partners. Wistfully, she watched as a man approached with exaggerated politeness to ask a girl to dance. They each held one end of a handkerchief. When they had danced awhile the man bowed and left her. She then tripped and pirouetted around until she saw a man to her liking and invited him to dance with her. Meanwhile, her late partner had approached another girl, and so it continued until almost everyone was on the floor—everyone except herself and a woman whose presence she did not suspect until she spoke behind her.

'It should be the tarantella that we dance in your presence—a dance connected with the poisonous spider the tarantula whose bite is said to be curable only by dancing so vigorously that its poison is sweated out of the body.'

Small hairs stood erect on the nape of Rosalba's neck as the venomous voice hissed in her ear. Grabbing courage with both hands, she remained perfectly still and without turning her head replied gently:

'I am sorry that you dislike me so much.'

'Dislike is a namby-pamby word—you Rossis are hated by us all!'

Rosalba bowed her head in acknowledgement of this fact. 'Yet a feud needs antagonists on either side to keep it alive. I do not feel antagonistic towards you or your people, I would like us to be friends.' She offered the olive branch tentatively, harbouring a hope that between this woman and herself the beginnings of a compromise might be reached. She was swiftly disillusioned by a harsh shout of laughter.

'If you are hoping to save your skin, *signorina*, you are wasting your time. The vendetta will continue until every Rossi has taken a last breath. There is only one way to stop the blood-letting and that is by arranging a marriage with one of our side, but there is no hope of that because there is not a man in this room who would partner you in a dance, much less a marriage!'

As if to prove her wrong, a young man swaggered towards them. He had obviously imbibed too much of the freely-available local wine, which was probably why he failed to distinguish Rosalba from the rest of the girls in similar dress. Besides that, as most of the girls were already dancing he had been left with very little choice.

When he bowed to her she scrambled to her feet and joined him, hoping to find anonymity among the crush of dancers. But it was not to be. Scandalised eyes bored into them, gradually a circle widened so that they were left isolated in the centre of the floor.

'Rossi! Rossi!' The sibilant hissing penetrated the young man's stupor. He halted, swaying stupidly, to peer into Rosalba's face. The musicians stopped playing and in the silence she could feel the crowd's malevolence pressing like a shroud around her. The boy felt it too. He stepped away as if to dissociate himself completely, then, his glazed eyes showing a flash of cunning, he swept a mocking bow and sneered.

'Salute, Goddess of Eryx!'

When a roar of laughter greeted his words he grinned, obviously feeling completely vindicated.

Bewildered by the ribaldry, Rosalba stood wistfully uncertain, clasping and unclasping her hands as jeers and catcalls decimated her courage. Renewed popularity went straight to the boy's head. Boldly he stepped forward. Her only warning was the blast of a garlic-laden breath before he bent to plunge his mouth upon hers, his clumsy fingers displacing the bodice of her shift so that one smooth pale shoulder was laid bare.

Her screams stifled, she began to fight, kicking and scratching with such puny strength her audience howled their amusement. The young herdsman became even more amorous, pulling her closer so that she was assailed by a strong smell of goats that was even more offensive than the garlic. Nauseated, she weakened, and the crowd, realising this, urged the boy on to inflict further indignities, mouthing crude suggestions, clamouring the name of Rossi with a ferocity that sounded to Rosalba like the baying of hounds after blood.

'*Cattivo babbuino!*' Never had she been more pleased to hear a familiar voice. Salvatore's exclamation sliced through their laughter. '*Buffone!* Put her down!'

He pushed the youth so hard he went staggering into the crowd, then grabbed Rosalba by the arm and held her in a torturing grip while his furious eyes raked the now silent watchers. 'It is important that she remains unharmed,' he blistered, 'until we have received the ransom.'

The downcast peasants sheepishly made way as he pushed her roughly towards the door. Once outside, he stopped to drag in several deep breaths of cold air, then he shook his head vigorously, in the manner of a dog casting off surplus water. To Rosalba's surprise, he stumbled as he stepped forward and a faint suspicion was confirmed when ruefully he admitted: 'I've drunk too much damned wine. Here, take my haversack, perhaps by the time we reach the cave I'll have regained my balance.'

The journey was accomplished in twice its usual time; Rosalba's emotions ravaged each step of the way with doubts about the wisdom of spending the night alone with a man whose taunting, derisory manner and glinting eyes held a promise of devilry.

She stumbled into the cave and huddled into a corner while he fumbled for matches to light the torch, wincing at clearly audible curses when the matches slipped through his fingers and he dropped to his knees to grope around the floor. As she curled into a frightened ball her hand subconsciously gripped a cold object sticking out of the haversack. It was round, smooth, and cold—*the tin of sleeping pills!*

Cautiously she withdrew it from the haversack, forcing her fingers to remain steady in case her movements should be betrayed by a tell-tale rattle. Cold sweat beaded her brow as she tightened her fingers and began unscrewing the top. At the first revolution it squeaked. She stopped, tense with fear, expecting Salvatore's swift reaction, but when his spate of cursing continued she urged herself to go on and sagged with relief when the lid slackened and came away in her hand. But the worst was not yet over. How many would be needed? Two? Three ...? Deciding that four would be a safer number she sidled them into her palm and slipped them into her apron pocket. She then replaced the lid and slid the tin back into the haversack.

She was leaning against the wall, shaking with reaction, when light flared inside the cave. She looked up, startled, and saw him towering over her with the blazing torch held aloft looking, to her terrified eyes, like some devil who had stepped straight out of Dante's Inferno.

'Goddess of Eryx!' he sneered, sending her spirits plummeting to the depths. 'Did you know that Aphrodite, Goddess of Love, patroness of prostitutes and courtesans, reputedly inhabited a temple on our own Mount Eryx where sailors, travellers, indeed any man in search of diversion, was certain of a welcome? Perhaps your young herdsman friend was privileged to receive from you a hint of encouragement—I cannot imagine why he should have likened you to her, otherwise. Sicilian girls are unfortunately not half so accommodating today as they were purported to be in the days of Aphrodite.'

She shrank from him. Wine had blunted finer feelings, had insulated his mind against the pinpricks of conscience, leaving him prey to the vices that were an integral part of every man, vices that lay like dregs submerged, but surged to the top at the slightest upset.

Torchlight flickered in the depths of his eyes as he bent down to threaten: 'I want to taste woman, woman, woman! Like an ant, I want to wallow in sugar ...' When he jerked her upwards into his arms a scream leapt to her lips, but was bitten back. He was beyond reason, her only means of salvation lay in the pocket of her apron; somehow she had to find a way to administer the pills.

Struggling to make her voice sound light, even playful, she offered: 'Would you like some more wine?'

'Why not?' He approved the suggestion. 'Let us turn our cave into a temple of Bacchus.'

Leaving him lolling against a wall, she picked up a flagon of wine and moved into deep shadow. She dared her fingers to fumble as she withdrew the pills from her pocket and transferred them to a goblet, crushing them against the base with a spoon. Then shakily she poured in the wine, splashing it in her eagerness to make certain he did not creep up behind her before the powder had been absorbed.

Her hands were still shaking when she handed him the goblet.

'Where's yours?'

'I don't want any,' she quavered.

'But I insist that you join me,' he insisted silkily.

'Very well.' She dared not argue in case he should offer to share his. 'I'll fetch another goblet.'

'Good.' He relaxed against the wall, prepared to wait until she joined him. Her teeth were chattering so much she dared not pretend to sip, but threw back her head and downed the lot in a series of panicky gulps.

'*Bravo!*' he approved, then to her intense relief followed suit. Wide-eyed, Rosalba watched his strong brown throat contracting with every swallow, praying that the powder had not had time to settle on the bottom, wondering if the drug would react upon him quickly or if it were one of the slow-acting kind whose effect would not be felt until after ...

Agitated, she jumped to her feet in an effort to interrupt a train of thought that had sent startled blood rushing through her veins. At the entrance to the cave she leant against a rock, turning hot cheeks up to the caress of a cool wind that was swirling dust all around her feet. It tugged at her sleeves, whipped the ends of her skirt and blew soft tendrils of hair into silver disarray.

Her back was turned towards him; his stealthy animal tread gave no warning of his approach as he crept up to trap her within a steely embrace. She froze to immobility when she was pulled tightly against a body that was hard, unyielding, insensitive as the granite nest that had been his birthplace. His lips impressed desire against the gentle curve of her neck and, much against her will, she reacted with a stab of ecstasy as his lips continued to probe.

The wind freshened, a gust teasing the hem of her skirt so that it billowed, then wrapped itself tightly around her legs.

'The breeze wants to be near you,' his throaty whisper turned her bones to water. 'It wants to brush your cheeks, to tease the hollow between your breasts ...' She panicked when lean fingers began untying the drawstring threaded through the neck of her blouse, but when she tried to resist he laughed and twirled her round to face him. 'It wants to know intimately every inviting, seductive curve of your body—*as I do*!'

He swung her off her feet and bore her effortlessly inside the cave. Even if she had had sufficient strength, it would have been pointless to struggle. Salvatore was a man possessed, a man consumed by such urgent need he was blind and deaf to reason.

He laid her on a sleeping bag stretched out on the ground. The torch had been extinguished, leaving the cave black as pitch, so that his eyes, glittering with triumph, reminded her of a jungle beast as he bore down upon her in the darkness.

'Toto, please don't ...!' she begged.

'So, it is Toto, is it?' he snarled a laugh. 'I am pleased to know that you, too, consider it is time for our friendship to progress.'

With his kiss he seemed to be endeavouring to purge himself of the bitter hatred he had been taught to feel for every Rossi. If a male member of her family had been reaping the bitter harvest of his vengeance he would probably have been beaten senseless, threatened with torture until he became crazed out of his mind. If a lash had been to hand his flesh might have been ribboned; with a knife deep, permanent reminders of Diavolo hatred might have been inflicted. But because she was a woman his torture, though equally painful, was more refined, a humiliating ordeal of kisses that scarred, caresses inflicted without emotion, sensitivity or tenderness.

She stopped fighting only when she realised how much she was adding to his enjoyment. Her mouth was bruised, her body lifeless, and Zia Giuseppina's beautiful costume lay a tattered heap on the floor when with a shuddering sigh of despair she went limp in his arms. She heard satisfied laughter deep in his throat and closed her eyes, biting deeply into her lip so that a scream would not betray her sensitive soul when she was forced to submit to his ultimate demands.

When the pressure of his body grew intolerably heavy she moaned. Suddenly his searching hands went still, his head dropped to lie a dead weight upon her breast. From somewhere she found sufficient strength to heave him away and instead of the resistance she had been expecting he rolled over and fell prone at her side. Suspecting trickery, she began inching out of his reach, then, as a thought struck her, she hesitated.

Cautiously, her heart thumping wildly, she leant over him, then choked back a sob of relief when she caught the heartening sound of a stertorous, heavily-drugged snore.

CHAPTER TEN

For what remained of the night Rosalba sat huddled near the entrance to the cave. Secure in the knowledge that Salvatore would remain unconscious for hours, she had fumbled in her suitcase for clothes to replace the skirt and top that lay, tattered as her emotions, on the floor of the cave. Wearily, her senses so numbed she moved like an automaton, she had pulled on the first garments that had come to hand before taking up her position, waiting for daylight so that she could find her way down the mountainside.

When pearly fingers of light began poking into the sky and the curtain of darkness slowly lifted she dragged her body erect and took a last look around the cave that had been the birthplace not only of a child destined to carry a burden of vengeance, but also of emotions too wild, too deep, too strong for a slight body which she had begun to believe existed merely to bear pain. She glanced once at Salvatore, her eyes tracing the strong, clean-cut features that looked peaceful in repose, the fiery eyes hooded by dark, thick-lashed lids, the taunting mouth relaxed into a half smile, the determined jaw cupped within lean brown fingers equally adept at healing and inflicting pain. She blinked back tears and moved away.

Outside it was almost light and as she began picking a way down the mountain she noticed movements on the plain below. Each day their searchers were out at first light, combing the whole of the countryside yet concentrating most of their efforts upon the area that Diavolo was known to favour. As she half-slithered, half-ran towards the foot of the mountain a shout rang out and she knew she had been spotted. Ten minutes later she was surrounded by arm-waving, gesticulating police and other grim-faced men whom she recognised as workers from her grandfather's estate. She was aware that she looked a sight in a dishevelled dress and with her hair all awry, but did not realise that it was her face—small, white and pinched, with dark crescent-shaped bruises beneath the eyes and cheeks bearing the marks of tears brushed away with a dusty hand—that had caused the men most concern.

'*Signorina*, are you hurt?'

'Where has that spawn of the devil been hiding you?'

'How did you manage to escape?'

'*Where is Diavolo?*'

This cry was taken up by dozens of bloodthirsty voices. 'Diavolo! Diavolo! Lead us to his hideout!'

Appalled by the thirst for vengeance expressed in ferocious shouts and expressions hard with hatred, Rosalba waved a vague hand and stammered:

'I'm sorry, I can't tell you ... Up there, there are so many caves, I have no idea which ...'

As their fanatical eyes lifted a man shouted and

pointed towards the mountain peak. Dozens of eyes
swung in the direction he was pointing, and
Rosalba's choked gasp was drowned by shouts of
triumph. Caught on a bush outside the cave, fluttering as if left to mark the spot, was Zia Giuseppina's
white apron, its passion-red flowers bursting with
brilliance as it was caught by the rays of a climbing
sun.

'Accompany the *signorina* to her grandfather's
home immediately,' the *capitano* rapidly ordered
one of his men, 'and inform the Conte,' he leered,
'that Diavolo will be handed over to him within
the hour!'

Her tearful entreaties that Diavolo should not be
hurt, that she should be allowed to stay, were
treated as hysteria and firmly brushed aside. 'Please
allow my driver to return you to your home,
signorina, your grandfather would be incensed were
I to inflict further distress by allowing you to wit-
ness the capture of a mad dog.'

Beginning vaguely to realise how much her
thoughtless flight had precipitated Salvatore into
danger, she began to sob, soft, heartbroken sobs
that continued all during the race towards Città del
Monte, so that by the time the driver was speeding
the car up the length of the castle drive, honking
his horn with great exuberance, her eyelids were
swollen, her cheeks raw, her mouth an uncontroll-
able quiver.

When the driver drew up with a flourish before
the steps leading up to the entrance, massive doors
swung open and simultaneously her grandfather
and Aprile stepped outside.

'Rosalba!' With a cry of relief Aprile dashed down the steps to greet her.

'*Managghia!*' After one venomously hissed word her grandfather stood stock-still, his hard eyes boring into Rosalba's face, probing, searching, questioning, as if, words having failed him, he could extract by telepathy all that he wanted to know.

She stared with repugnance, reminded of the deadly cobra, as his tense body stretched to its full height with head rearing, tongue darting, fang-swift, between lips dangerously thinned.

'*Dio!*' he spat, cold eyes flickering over a possession of his that had been stolen, 'someone shall pay heavily for this!' Then, belatedly remembering that vengeance should be a secondary consideration, he rushed down the stairs to clasp her in his arms. '*Mia cara nipotina,*' he murmured, 'I would have given anything to spare you such an experience. Come, let us get you up to your room. We must talk, but first of all you must rest. Aprile!' he rasped, 'attend to your cousin, see that she has a warm bath, some food, everything that she needs, before you put her to bed.'

'But I don't want to go to bed!' Panic loosened Rosalba's tongue. 'I must know what's going to happen to Salvatore. Please, Grandfather, promise me that he won't be harmed, he's not to blame ...'

'*Silence!*' His taut command cut through her words. Great strain and utmost control were evident as he bit out: 'Diavolo abducted you from my home, had the audacity to enter my room and leave a ransom note beside my bed, yet you are foolish enough to plead for him, to try to absolve him from blame!

What ails you, child, has the devil turned your head!'

She almost crumpled beneath a weight of despair. By attempting to intercede she had made matters worse. This was not the time, she should have waited until tempers had had time to cool. Yet she dared not wait too long, for in less than an hour, the *capitano* had promised, Salvatore would be brought to the castle—for his safety's sake, it was imperative that she should be present when he arrived.

Employing brave diplomacy, she whispered: 'I'm sorry, Grandfather. I'll have a bath, and some food, as you suggested, then afterwards could we please talk?'

'Not until you are completely rested,' he curtly declined. 'Aprile,' he flicked a compelling finger, 'kindly take your cousin up to her room.'

Aprile babbled incessant questions while a maid ran Rosalba's bath, but she was too dispirited to supply more than cursory answers; her mind was concentrated upon the cave, wondering if Salvatore had roused from his drugged sleep in time to escape, or if he had not, whether he was being roughly treated.

'Rosalba, for heaven's sake, have you been struck dumb!' Aprile's querulous question penetrated her agonised mind. 'You've been missing for over a week, spirited away from beneath our very noses by the nephew of a notorious bandit, held captive in a mountain cave while the police and every man employed on the estate has been scouring the countryside looking for you. Grandfather has been demented, I've been worried sick, yet when you finally arrive back you reply to my questions in monosyllables! What's he like, this bandit, Diavolo? I can still hardly believe such a thing is possible—we ought to have listened when you insisted that you were being followed, but your tale sounded too far-fetched to be true. Never again will I be cynical,' she promised, running a comb through Rosalba's hair, 'in future I shall bear in mind what Grandfather told me when at first I pooh-poohed the idea of abduction and suggested that the ransom note was someone's idea of a joke. "Such actions may be inconceivable in Britain," he told me sourly, "but here in Sicily anything is possible."'

It was a relief to escape into the bathroom, to be free of Aprile's insatiable curiosity, to have time to think, to decide which way to approach her grandfather with an aim to ending the savage vendetta that had no place among civilised people. Both Salvatore and her grandfather were unreasonable men, she mused with puckered brow, yet neither lacked intelligence, and so it was to their intelligence she must appeal by pointing out that there is nothing sacred about convention, no honour in giving in to primitive passions or continuing with outmoded customs. 'Intellect will annul fate,' she assured herself, yet her eyes remained troubled. 'All that's needed is for both men to exercise a little restraint. It shouldn't be impossible to persuade them both to curb their grudges, bury their animosity so that, perhaps, they might some day become friends.'

She towel-dried her hair, slipped into a simple

dress made of pink cotton, then sat at an open window so that sunshine and a light breeze could dry her hair into a wavy cap of silver. She toyed with the food that had been brought to her room on a tray, her appetite blunted by worry, her ears attentive for the least sound that might warn her of Salvatore's arrival.

She did not have long to wait. Her first indication was the sound of vehicles rumbling up the driveway before a cavalcade of lorries appeared, all tightly packed with men, with at its head a jeep carrying the widely-grinning police captain in its passenger seat and in its rear seat Salvatore, flanked by two policemen, each sitting with a gun trained in his direction. Rosalba's fork clattered from nerveless fingers as she jumped up, ran out of the bedroom and careered wildly down the stairs, erupting into the hallway just as her grandfather strode from his study.

The first thing Salvatore saw as he was pushed through the main entrance was the arrogant Conte holding his trembling granddaughter within a protective arm. He was not to know that the arm was acting as a restraint or that warning fingers were gouging into her shoulder to prevent her from running towards him.

Rosalba stared at the bruise standing out livid against his cheek, at a brown shoulder showing bare through the tatters of a shirt that had been intact when she had left him, and at blood slowly trickling from the corner of his tightly-compressed mouth.

'What have they done to you!' Her constricted

whisper was drowned by the captain's strident exclamation.

'Here, Signor Conte,' he helped Salvatore forward with a hard shove, 'is the renegade Diavolo!'

Rosalba sensed her grandfather's triumph, felt satisfaction oozing from his very fingertips.

'So!' he hissed with frightening sibilance. '*You* are Diavolo! Even without an introduction I would have recognised you anywhere as a branch of the same rotten family tree that nurtured the outlaw Turiddu—the same looks, the same audacity, the same lack of wisdom that led you both to tilt at my authority. As you seem determined to ape your late uncle, it shall be my pleasure to ensure that you enjoy a similar fate.'

'To suffer a traitorous betrayal you mean?' For a second Salvatore's glance flickered over Rosalba. 'To be ambushed and shot in the back by one of your cowardly minions?' He jerked erect, his injured mouth twisted into a line of mockery. 'You, too, run true to form, Signor Conte—like the reptile you are reputed to resemble, you are cold-blooded, venomous, and deadly.'

Rosalba could stand no more. This was not the way she had intended the encounter to go. Instead of reason there was hatred, instead of tolerance they were displaying an intolerable thirst for revenge.

'Stop it, both of you!' She pulled out of her grandfather's grasp and ran to a spot midway between the two of them. Fixing pleading eyes first upon one and then the other, she appealed: 'Don't you think this stupid vendetta has gone on long enough? You owe a duty, both of you, to those who look to you for leadership. How can you abuse your positions of trust by setting such a dreadful example to un-educated people who know no better—who never *will* know better so long as you persist in ranging family against family simply to satisfy your own vindictive egos? A leader is a man who accepts responsibilities, *so be responsible*,' she charged fiercely, 'admit that you've been wrong in the past, wipe all thoughts of vengeance from your minds so that you can begin again—as friends!'

She knew she had lost when they both stared as if at someone insane.

'I'll admit to only one wrong,' her grandfather told her thinly, 'and that is that I omitted to ensure that his family was annihilated completely. For-tunately, that is an error that can be corrected im-mediately. All that needs to be decided is which method to choose. Have you a preference, Signor Diavolo?' he mocked his contemptuous adversary.

'Do your damnedest!' Salvatore challenged, his erect body, flashing eyes and proud features project-ing dark, satanic contempt.

'Very well,' the Conte acceded graciously, 'the *bastinado*, then.' With the assurance of a feudal lord, he instructed the captain of police: 'You have done your duty well, Capitano, there is no need for you to become further involved—all that remains is for you to report back to your chief that, so far as the authorities are concerned, the matter is now closed. My own men will see to it that justice is done.'

Rosalba did not believe that such flagrant de-spotism could be overlooked until the policemen actually began trooping out of the hall. The sound of their cars receding into the distance was a mere humming in her ears when the men over whom her grandfather wielded such power that they even obeyed his orders to kill seized Salvatore by the arms and began pushing and prodding him outside.

'Wait!' Her command sounded faint in her own ears, yet it must have been audible, because the men halted.

'Well?' Her grandfather's smile was salve-smooth. 'There is something you wish to say to this villain before he is taken away?'

She swallowed hard. Lies did not come easily to her tongue, but if the statement so firmly made by the peasant woman last evening were to be believed, there remained just one slim chance of saving his life, so she did not hesitate.

Even so, she could not bring herself to tell an outright lie, merely to prevaricate. 'Grandfather, what if I should be pregnant? How would you feel, knowing that you'd ordered the death of the father of my unborn child?'

Her words seemed to bounce from the walls, then rise to linger like a doom-laden echo among the nooks and crannies of the timbered ceiling. The effect upon her listeners was shocking—a pregnant pause, she thought, nervously suppressing a rise of giggling hysteria.

The faces of the estate workers reddened and they began shuffling awkwardly, debating whether to follow their instincts and flee out of the presence of the Conte's incredulous rage, or to remain until they received his order to leave. His face was grey, his white-knuckled hands clasping and unclasping as he fought for mastery over scandalised disbelief.

The extent of his rage left Rosalba feeling strangely unconcerned. In the beginning he had wielded powerful fear, but after her ordeal of the past few days, during which she had faced horrors that a mere week ago would have sent her screaming with fright, opposing her grandfather seemed comparatively tame. She had creatures of the wild to thank for her new-found courage, daily contact with a host of reptiles and insects had taught her to revise her thinking so that she was now able to view them as mere nuisances. Courage erupts when courage is needed. The reptiles had been everywhere, especially the lizards, big and small, brown and green, and one particularly obscene species Salvatore had called a gecko that had a huge head, colourless body and legs astraddle like a crocodile's. Long, black snakes had slithered among the stones and flying insects had threatened to become entangled in her hair, bright butterflies, huge dragonflies, hornets, grasshoppers and, of course, the myriad ants. But her greatest triumph had been her mastery of fear of physical contact—man, the greatest animal of all, had been an unknown quantity, yet, as with the lesser species, constant proximity had reduced her fear and replaced it with a vibrant, pulsating emotion which she now recognised as love.

Her tender glance swung towards Salvatore and remained riveted upon features set hard as granite. He was white to the lips, his eyes—the only part of him that seemed alive—dark glinting pools mirroring a stunned incredulity she found puzzling until she remembered that he probably had a very vague recollection of the previous night and that the little he could recall was no doubt lending credence to her story. She wanted to run to him, to assure him that last night, although the intent had been present, his actions had not been consummated, but she dared not. For the time being, at least, he must continue to believe what her grandfather so obviously believed.

The Conte looked every year of his age when, with a listless hand, he waved his workmen outside. If looks could inflict physical injury, Salvatore would have been stabbed to the heart when the Conte trained his eyes upon the man he believed had violated his granddaughter's innocence.

'You will marry Rosalba, of course.' He spoke without bluff or pretence, making the plain statement a threat that acted upon Salvatore like a spur.

His proud head jerked erect and though he still seemed shaken his voice held a ring of contempt. 'For me to take a Rossi in marriage would require a very powerful incentive.'

'You have one.' The Conte's reply was deadly earnest. 'Either you marry or you die.'

Desperately, Rosalba tried to catch Salvatore's eye in an effort to communicate that such fencing was unnecessary, that the situation had been created as a ploy to save his life, but he seemed deliberately to avoid looking her way.

'Some would say that death might be preferable,' he iced.

'That can be arranged!' The Conte's contorted

features registered bitter hatred. 'And yet, in spite of the fact that my men will be told to say nothing of what they have learned today, I have not the least doubt that within days the whole village, if not the whole island, will be conversant with the fact that my granddaughter is pregnant. Therefore, although I loathe the idea of any grandchild of mine bearing your name, I will admit that Diavolo is just slightly preferable to *bastardo*!'

Rosalba recoiled from the ugly word. The situation was getting completely out of hand—the two were like horses with bits between their teeth, stampeding hatred raced between them. Sworn antagonists, neither intended to give an inch.

Salvatore, sounding once more completely controlled, stressed with a lift of an eyebrow: 'There is no guarantee that a child exists.'

'No,' the Conte breathed heavily, unused to being dominated, 'that is true. Although it goes against my instincts to accept the word of a villain, in this case I am prepared to do so. Can you swear to me that the possibility does not exist?'

Dull colour rose beneath Salvatore's tan. He hesitated fractionally—then, glancing quickly at Rosalba, he conceded grimly: 'No, unfortunately, I cannot.'

Standing at a wistful distance, she eyed them, knowing that one word from herself could put an end to the farce, the duel of temperaments, yet equally aware that a denial would be equivalent to a sentence of death. The atmosphere was electrifying as the contest of nerves and words continued, neither man entirely confident yet each determined to stand his ground.

'I'll tell you what I am prepared to do.' The Conte sounded weary. 'In your ransom note you demanded, in exchange for my granddaughter, that a fully equipped hospital should be built for the exclusive use of your mountain dwellers, and also that a trust fund should be set up to finance its up-keep. On the day of your wedding,' he promised slowly, 'I shall instruct that the building of such a hospital is to commence.'

Rosalba saw a satisfied glint spring to Salvatore's eyes. She winced, feeling herself an object of barter.

'And the trust fund . . .?' he prompted the Conte. 'A hospital is useless without sufficient money to run it.'

'The fund will be set up on the day that my grandchild is born.'

Rosalba's cheeks burned while Salvatore took time to consider the offer. It made little difference to her whether he accepted or declined, for she had no intention of marrying a man who had to be black-mailed into considering her as a bride. Yet in spite of the fact that the situation was purely hypothetical she experienced a thrill of delicious terror when, with a reluctance she found galling, he submitted.

'Very well, Conte Rossi. Providing you comply with the agreed terms, I will marry your grand-daughter.'

CHAPTER ELEVEN

THE following days developed into an unbelievable nightmare for Rosalba. Seconds after Salvatore had agreed to marry her she had been whisked out of his sight and had not been allowed so much as a glimpse of him since.

According to Aprile, he was housed somewhere in the castle—she did not know where exactly—being watched day and night in case he should change his mind and try to escape. Aprile had not been told any of the details, only that a marriage had been arranged, and although Rosalba felt in urgent need of a *confidente* she mistrusted her cousin's babbling tongue and dared not risk acquainting her with the facts in case the truth should reach her grandfather's ears.

Many times she was tempted to confess her lie, especially when she discovered that her grandfather, by dint of pulling every available string, had managed to arrange for the wedding ceremony to take place in a matter of days. To her surprise, he seemed to have come to terms with the situation and had even, by some devious route of mind, arrived at a stage bordering upon satisfaction.

The reason for this became evident the day he sought her out and began outlining his plans. She was pacing her room, wondering desperately how she could manage a vital conversation with Salvatore, when a knock sounded on the door and in answer to her request to enter, her grandfather stepped inside. He had a habit, she had noticed, of massaging invisible oil into his palms whenever he felt pleased.

'Rosalba, my dear,' he accepted her invitation to sit and took time to adjust an immaculate crease in his trousers, 'I have come to acquaint you with the progress that has been made. A licence has been obtained and the wedding day is fixed for three days from today. The ceremony will take place in the family church, but because of the ... er ... circumstances prevailing,' he looked uncomfortable, then hurried on, 'no guests have been invited, although the estate workers will be given a holiday and will no doubt gather outside the church to proffer their good wishes to the newlyweds. I hope you don't mind,' he strove to sound apologetic, yet Rosalba suspected he cared little whether she minded or she did not, 'but as there has not been time to have a wedding dress specially made I have instructed Rita to unearth the dress worn by your grandmother on her wedding day. If my memory serves me correctly, her measurements were similar to yours, and as your grandmother was blessed with impeccable taste I'm certain you will be delighted with her choice.'

Rosalba jumped to her feet, unable to conceal her agitation. Granted, it had been her action that had precipitated the marriage, but for the sole purpose of staying her grandfather's hand. She had given no thought to the consequence, but even if she had her imagination would have led her no further than an immediate ceasing of hostilities and a few uncomfortable days of sham betrothal, during which time Salvatore would be able to effect his escape and she would afterwards return to England, her holiday over, where the trauma of the past week would fade from her mind until it was reduced to no more than an incredible memory.

'Grandfather . . .' she paced nervously, searching for words. 'I need more time—I know that might sound strange considering how f-friendly Salvatore and I have become, but the truth of the matter is he's almost a stranger to me!'

'My dear,' he spread his hands in a deprecatory manner, 'time is the one thing you cannot have.'

She knew he was referring to the supposed birth, so she had no choice but to argue. 'In modern society it's no longer considered essential to marry before the birth of a child. Today many couples wait, sometimes for years, before making up their minds as to whether or not they're suited.'

She tensed to combat his cold scrutiny. 'None of our family has ever been born out of wedlock,' he told her coldly, 'and so long as it is within my power to prevent it none ever will. Diavolo is not an ideal choice,' he eyed her with plain dislike, 'but as a strong and healthy sire he will do.'

Rosalba blanched from the crudity of the remark. Here was proof, if she needed it, of his fanatical devotion to the continuity of his line. Sadly, she reproved. 'You never learn from your mistakes, do you, Grandfather? Once before you tried to force a marriage between my father and Salvatore's mother, and the result was a vendetta that has continued to this very day.'

'Your father was a fool.' He stood up, shedding all pretence of benevolence. 'He was a simpleton like his mother who kept her brain in her heart. Diavolo, in spite of his faults, possesses all the fire and passion of his race; in your veins runs the blood of a proud aristocratic family that has survived for generations —such a combination will, I hope, provide me with a grandson worthy of the Rossi image.'

The gloves were off. Tired of having to parade uncharacteristic emotions of paternal affection, he was declaring ruthless intent, confident that he held the upper hand.

Hating his complacency, his complete disregard for the feeling of others, she stammered a reckless refusal.

'I will not be coerced into marriage, Grandfather!'

She managed not to cringe when he turned upon her a look of implacable determination.

'In three days' time,' he spelled out slowly, 'you will join Diavolo at the altar. You will either leave the church as his bride—or as an accomplice to what you insist upon referring to as his murder.'

For a stunned half hour after he had left she paced her room, searching until her mind was exhausted for a way of escape from the seemingly inextricable tangle. Defeat was hard to accept. Having lived in a world within which freedom of the individual was taken for granted, she found it almost impossible to come to terms with the fact that in some isolated areas of this small, neglected island feudalism still flourished to the extent that one despotic old man had the power to decide the destiny of simple uneducated people who had been conditioned to regard him as some kind of minor deity. The indolent, ruthless manner in which her grandfather had passed sentence upon Salvatore was proof that the taking of life presented him with no qualms. But then, as she had been shocked to discover earlier, Sicilians as a race were not unduly bothered by conscience. Attempting to justify the actions of her bandit son, Zia Giuseppina had told her airily:

'Murder is commonplace in our land.' Then, reading alarm in Rosalba's widening eyes she had hastened to reassure. 'Do not worry, *signorina*, foreigners such as yourself are quite safe, we murder only during vendettas and quarrels.'

Wearily, Rosalba discarded the argument that her grandfather's threat to kill Salvatore had been no more than bluff. With any other race, in any other country, the possibility could exist, but, as he had so rightly affirmed to Aprile, *in Sicily anything can happen.*

Abruptly, her nervous pacing ceased as she faced the appalling fact that the decision had been made for her—if Salvatore's life were to be saved she would have to go through with the marriage ceremony. She would, of course, explain to him that responses made under duress would be rendered meaningless, leaving them entirely uncommitted, and that once out of reach of her grandfather's authority they could part amicably and go their different ways.

Her mind made up, she went in search of Rita, glad of the diversion offered by positive action. She found her hovering in the passageway outside her room.

'Rita, my grandfather tells me——'

'*Sì, signorina*,' Rita interrupted in a nervous rush, 'I have been waiting for you.' She seemed agitated, her fingers clasping and unclasping around an ornate key. In response to an enquiring look, she proffered the key with a haste that suggested to Rosalba that she was glad to be rid of it. 'It unlocks the door of the Contessa's room. Since her death, no one has set foot inside.'

'Not even to dust?' Rosalba's eyebrows rose. 'But why—don't tell me you're afraid of ghosts?'

An expression of superstitious fear tightened the housekeeper's features. Sketching a hasty sign of the cross, she backed away mumbling: 'The souls of the unhappy linger for a long time after death. The Contessa was never seen to smile, not even on the day she arrived here as a bride.'

Rosalba shivered, able to understand why. Taking pity on the old woman whose eyes were riddled with fear, she consoled: 'Very well, Rita, the wedding dress shouldn't be hard to find, I'll search for it alone.'

Rita bobbed a swift, relieved curtsey, but as she turned to flee a thought struck Rosalba.

'Rita, do you have keys to all the rooms in the castle?'

'*Sì, signorina*.' She waited.

'Then could you,' Rosalba's tongue flicked round suddenly dry lips, 'could you get me the key to Signor Diavolo's room?'

Terror flashed into Rita's eyes. She backed away.

'I dare not, *signorina*, the Conte would kill me if he were to find out!'

'But he need never know,' Rosalba urged insistently, 'and it's imperative that I speak with Signor Diavolo—I wouldn't take more than a few minutes, I promise you.'

Rita hesitated, obviously in a turmoil of doubt, her eyes darting around the passageway as if she expected her employer's avenging spirit to materialise out of the granite-grey walls. Rosalba's suspicion that her grandfather inspired little affection in his retainers was confirmed when Rita stepped close to confide in a tense whisper: 'Because of your likeness to the Contessa whom we all adored I will do as you ask. But stay no longer than five minutes, I beg of you; the Conte has spies everywhere—servants who have offended him in the past have been punished so severely that now no one dares to cross him. Promise that you will be careful, *signorina*,' she trembled, 'for if you are caught he will know immediately who it was that gave you the key!'

'Don't worry, Rita,' Rosalba gave her a reassuring hug, 'I will not allow you to suffer on my account.'

Seeming only slightly relieved, Rita muttered in rapid undertone: 'Tonight the Conte is dining with friends. As soon as he leaves the castle the servants will relax and gather together in the kitchen for supper, and that is the time you will be least likely to be seen slipping into the *signore*'s room. It is on the ground floor, near to the kitchen; when the coast is clear I will fetch you the key.'

'Thank you, Rita, I——' but Rita was scurrying along the passageway with a speed indicative of panic brought about by her own daring.

With an optimistic spring in her step, Rosalba approached the door Rita had indicated, turned the key in the lock, and stepped inside what had been her grandmother's private suite of rooms. An eerie, ghostlike atmosphere struck her immediately she entered. She hesitated, fighting rising panic, but forced herself to pick her way between items of furniture shrouded in dustcovers until she reached the window where she flung open the shutters, allowing sunshine to flood the room, transforming its tomblike qualities, allowing her a glimpse of tasteful decor and to sense the beauty-loving aura that had existed in the room created by a woman who had surrounded herself with an abundance of material wealth in an attempt to compensate a spirit starved of affection and joy.

One by one, as covers were removed, she unearthed pieces of priceless furniture and ornaments —brocaded chairs; dainty tables; exquisite porcelain images of animals and birds so lifelike she had to touch them to convince herself they were not real. As she traced the outline of a tiny, blue-plumaged bird perched upon the limb of a tree she thought it seemed poised to fly at any moment out of the open window and wondered if her grandmother's choice of ornament was indicative of an urge to be free, if she, in common with these small, wild creatures, had been a thing of beauty trapped inside the cold grey stone of the mountain upon which the castle and surrounding village had been built.

'Poor Nonna Rossi,' she murmured, 'why did you never smile?' As if pulled by invisible strings her hands reached out towards a bureau fashioned out of wood the colour of honey, satin-sheened, with slender gold handles on each drawer. In spite of years of disuse, when she tugged the drawer slid out noiselessly and smoothly, exposing neat piles of lace-trimmed handkerchiefs embroidered with the Rossi crest, each bearing her grandmother's personal initial. With a start, she recalled that she and her grandmother shared the same name. She picked up one of the handkerchiefs and as tentatively she lifted it to her cheek a dried-up rose petal fluttered out of its folds, distintegrating into dust as it settled on the base of the drawer. Words read once, many years ago, rose to the surface of her mind. She heard them breathed in a sad, gentle tone she did not recognise as her own.

'The rose distils a healing balm
The beating pulse of pain to calm.'

'Did marriage to Grandfather bring you no happiness at all, Nonna?' she sighed.

Once more obeying a strong compulsion, she undid the clasp of a flat leather wallet she saw tucked into the corner of the drawer and when she opened it the reply to her question stared from the framed photographs of two children, a boy and a girl, whom she had no difficulty in recognising as her father and his sister Caterina.

Shaking off the feeling that she had somehow communicated with the dead, she shut the drawer and moved across the room to slide open the door of a wardrobe entirely covering one wall of the room. Its contents were protected by covers, each item cocooned in a silken bag sealed at the bottom with a row of tiny stitches. Guided only by touch, she worked her way through stiff brocades, fine cottons, heavy coats and bulky furs, discarding the most unlikely items and setting aside those that felt promising. With the aid of a small pair of scissors unearthed from a sewing box, she undid a few stitches from the bottom of each bag—sufficient only to make an opening large enough to display its contents—and at her third attempt uncovered a square of ivory-coloured lace. Carefully, she snipped across the row of stitches, rolled up the protective bag, and slipped it off the hanger.

The dress rustled and sighed as she spread it across a couch before taking a step backward to capture the full effect of hand-worked lace ivoried with age yet still retaining its original virgin beauty. Long sleeves terminated in a point above each cuff, the neckline was primly demure, and the very full skirt was gathered finely at the waist to fall in soft folds over an underskirt of paper-crisp taffeta. A cloud of ivory tulle attached to a headdress of tiny seed pearls completed an outfit that made her heart flutter at the thought of wearing it—knowing that its ethereal elegance would barely be adequate concealment for shaking limbs and madly erratic heartbeats when she faced the black-devil stare of a bridegroom who felt nothing but hatred for his bride. Filled with sudden revulsion, she spun on her heel and ran from the room, leaving behind the dress that destiny had decreed was never to be worn by an adored and happy bride.

As evening drew near she waited in a fever of

impatience for her grandfather to leave the castle. As Aprile was spending the day in Palermo and had indicated that she would be late home, Rosalba had a tray sent up to her room and sat picking at her solitary meal with one ear cocked for the sound of her grandfather's limousine drawing up in front of the castle.

It seemed an eternity had passed before she heard him thanking Alessandro for assisting him into the car. As soon as she heard the soft slam of the door and then the purring of the powerful engine she flew out of her room, down the stairs and across the hall to ease open the massive front door, where she peeped through a chink until the tail lights of the limousine had disappeared from sight.

Feeling incredibly keyed up, she prowled the empty hall, mentally urging Rita to hurry, but it was a good ten minutes later before the old house-keeper opened a door and stood on the threshold beckoning her towards the kitchens. Holding a warning finger to her lips, she urged Rosalba to tread softly as she began leading the way down a passageway, passed enclosed kitchen quarters, and stopped outside a door, set apart from the rest, bearing a huge lock on a surface that looked substantial enough to guard the entrance to a dungeon.

Rita had to use both hands to insert the massive key she had kept hidden beneath her apron. 'The *signore* is housed in a disused storeroom,' she whispered apologetically. 'The interior is comfortless, but I have seen to it that he has been well fed.'

'Thank you, Rita,' Rosalba patted her shoulder

with a surprisingly shaky hand, 'I'll be as quick as I can.'

The lock was well oiled so the key turned with the merest click. Not even hinges squeaked as she pushed open the door and slipped inside the room. Salvatore was lying fully dressed on top of a bunk, his dark head bent over a book held close to a flickering oil lamp. Though she made little noise, he looked up immediately she entered, his eyes piercing the gloom, seeking the identity of the intruder. Before she could speak he reacted, gathered muscles projecting him in one lithe leap across the space dividing them.

She was staring, appalled, at bare stone walls and floor, at a coarse wooden table and one rickety chair, when his hands gripped her shoulders. Eyes wide with distress swung his way.

'I'm sorry,' she choked, 'I had no idea you were living in such dreadful conditions.'

Whatever he had been about to say died in his throat as, with eyebrows winging, he cast a surprised glance around the room.

'I have existed in worse places,' he shrugged, then, his jaw clamped, he released her shoulders and moved away. 'And so have you. In the cave, for instance . . .'

There was so much she wanted to say and so little time to say it, yet at the mention of the cave she allowed herself to be sidetracked. 'I had nothing to do with your capture! I didn't lead the police to the cave—they caught sight of the apron that had been accidentally left outside when I made my esscape.'

'You have no need to apologise.' His voice was harsh. 'You were perfectly entitled to your revenge. I behaved in a despicable manner.'

She stared at his grim outline, at squared-off shoulders, rigid back, and tensely-muscled thighs. She had imagined him to be entirely without compassion, yet his voice was full of bitter self-condemnation when, keeping his back turned towards her, he continued his strangled apology.

'I'm damned if I can understand what happened to me that night! I had drunk a few glasses of wine—a couple too many, with hindsight—yet on previous occasions I have drunk much more without suffering such deadly effect. I do not expect you to believe me when I say that the last thing I intended was to inflict harm—*especially*,' when he thumped a clenched fist into his palm she jerked away, startled by this evidence of impotent anger, of bitter regret, '*not harm of that sort!*'

'Toto . . .!' she gasped, overwhelmed with distress on his behalf. She had done this to him! With a few thoughtless yet well-meaning words she had deeply offended his code of ethics, had lacerated his self-respect, smashed his pride. '*Please*, don't torment yourself—you did nothing . . .'

'*Nothing!*' He spun round to wither her with a blast from blazing eyes. 'Has your liberated society conditioned you to regard even rape as being of little consequence?'

His contempt stung tears into her eyes. 'But you *did* nothing,' she sobbed, stamping her foot in an excess of frustration.

Further protest was silenced by a look of hard

dislike. 'I admit that I was inebriated,' he told her stonily, 'so inebriated that I passed out for the first time in my life, but there are some things that I remember clearly—so clearly that they will be branded for ever on my conscience. For instance,' he cruelly reminded her, 'the thrill and delight of pinning your naked, struggling body beneath mine; the taste of lips sweetened by wine; your sobs and urgent, impassioned pleas for mercy. Beyond that, my mind is blank, but not my powers of reason that tell me that no man's body is capable of reaching such a pitch of emotion without demanding the relief of ultimate fulfilment. If I were a true apostle of the vendetta,' he confessed, his eyes now bleak, 'I would rejoice in the fact that I had taken a true barbarian's revenge upon the granddaughter of my enemy. But it seems that my years among the civilised have made a greater impact than I had imagined. I have become soft, the savage in me is all but tamed. Yet not tamed enough to cower whenever your grandfather cracks the whip,' his head tilted, a little of his pride returning. 'Honour demanded that I should marry you, yet he was given no inkling that I had already resigned myself to this fate. I made the old snake squirm, did I not?' Tight lips parted in a mirthless smile. 'He met my ransom demands, so my people will benefit; that fact alone will help lighten the weight of my shackles.'

Well-married, a man is winged—ill-matched, he is shackled!

Unaware of the proverb running through Rosalba's mind, he misinterpreted her wince. 'You are apprehensive about playing the role of Satan's angel?' he queried with a wry twist of the lips. 'We have a belief in this country that all the best marriages begin with a little aversion. Console yourself with the thought that if this is so, then ours should develop into a bed of roses.'

An agitated rap upon the door forestalled her reply. It was Rita urging her to hurry. Exercising the highest female grace, Rosalba remained silent as she made her way towards the door, too disheartened to indulge in even one backward look. She had tried to speak, but Salvatore had refused to listen, and now her fountain of words had run dry— she did not quite know whether because she cared too little or too much.

CHAPTER TWELVE

APRILE'S questions had become more and more demanding as her anxiety grew. That she was also very hurt was obvious when she burst into Rosalba's room on the morning of her wedding day to accuse, wide-eyed with disbelief:

'I've been told that your wedding is to take place *today*, yet you gave me no inkling. I, it seems, am the last one to be told! How could you treat me so, your own cousin, your best friend ...? And what about your mother, shouldn't she be here?'

Rosalba's slight figure braced. She had put off telling Aprile until the last possible moment, afraid that the inevitable arguments might weaken her shaky resolve, but now the moment she had dreaded had arrived. Subconsciously imitating a gladiator girding his loins, she tightened the belt of her dressing gown around a tiny waist and drew herself erect. Daring her voice to tremble, she strove to sound calm and unconcerned.

'I'm sorry, Aprile, if my secretive attitude has offended you. I wanted you to know, but I knew you wouldn't approve, and you must admit,' she managed a slight smile, 'that you can be a very eloquent opponent! You'd better sit down,' wearily she waved her cousin towards a chair. 'What I'm about to tell you is rather shocking.'

Quick to sense that Rosalba was under intolerable strain, Aprile obeyed without argument and steeled herself not to interrupt as Rosalba faltered through the startling tale, beginning with her encounter with Salvatore in the market-place, touching only lightly upon the days they had spent together in the cave, and ending with the admission that in order to save his life she had told a tremendous lie.

Aprile's face was as ashen as her cousin's by the time she had finished speaking. Incredulity deepened her wide eyes to black as they searched Rosalba's face, hoping for some hint that she was being made the victim of a tremendous leg-pull. When reluctantly she had to conclude that she was not, she expelled a long, slow breath, then croaked:

'Salvatore feels bound to marry you because you implied that there's a possibility that you might be prcgnant, in which case,' she continued slowly, 'he must have grounds for suspecting you were speaking the truth, otherwise he would have denied responsibility.'

'I tricked him,' Rosalba confessed, her cheeks fiery with embarrassment as she met her cousin's accusing eyes. 'Circumstances were such that he could have ... he was prepared to ...' she stumbled, then gave up, knowing she could leave the rest to Aprile's sharp intuition. 'Anyway,' she rushed on, 'he didn't, because I dosed him with sleeping pills and he passed out.'

'At the psychological moment, I gather.' Aprile's tone was dry. 'Poor man, if I weren't so angry with him I could feel sympathy for one prepared to accept punishment even though he only suspects that he's guilty. Have you considered what might happen when he discovers, as he certainly must, that you've lied to him? You're not dealing with an English gentleman, Rosalba. Diavolo is so darned *maschio* he frightens me—I should have thought the very idea of marriage to such a man would terrify *you*.'

When a small, secretive smile curved Rosalba's lips Aprile's patience snapped. Jumping to her feet, she rounded upon her unworldly cousin, angered by her naïveté, an anger accelerated by an uncomfortable feeling that in some way she herself might be to blame. 'Rosalba, please be realistic! I know I urged you to cast off your inhibitions, but not to this extent! Let's go home,' she urged, 'now, this very minute, without even waiting to pack our bags. All we'll need is a passport each—we'll get to the airport somehow!'

'I can't,' Rosalba refused quietly. 'Salvatore's life will be forfeit.'

'Damn Salvatore!' Displaying a totally Latin gesture, Aprile flung her arms in the air. 'And damn Grandfather and every other of his superstition-riddled race—let them kill one another if they want to, their stupid vendettas are no concern of ours!'

Much to Aprile's dread, Rosalba's expression set into lines of stubbornness. In one last furious bid to make her see reason, she aimed a jab at her conscience. 'And what about your mother, how do you suppose she'll feel when she discovers that her only daughter was in such haste she couldn't wait for her to attend her marriage to a stranger?'

'Don't ...!' Rosalba turned away to hide features quivering with hurt. 'Things are bad enough without——'

'Believe me, they'll get worse!' Aprile fiercely interrupted. 'Have you stopped to think what life will be like among people whose strange manners and customs are comprehensible only to themselves? The word love is missing from their vocabulary. Marriage to them is a business deal in which the amount of the bride's dowry is of paramount importance. My mother has told me many times of their peculiar marriage customs—the way in which the question of the amount to be contributed by the bride is raised immediately the betrothal has been settled and of how, to make things even more businesslike, a professional valuer is employed to assess the value of the bride's contribution. Indeed, at this very moment, there is in Grandfather's study an old crone who turned up on the doorstep this morning claiming to be Diavolo's aunt and saying that she'd come to negotiate for the marriage in place of his mother. Normally, her call would have been paid to *your* mother with the object of ascertaining firstly whether Diavolo's attentions were acceptable and secondly what dowry the bride would be bringing. As your mother is absent, however, she's agreed to haggle with Grandfather, and by the looks of her I'd say he has more than met his match.'

'That will be Zia Giuseppina!' Aprile was amazed by Rosalba's evident pleasure. 'Oh, I'm so pleased she was able to come!'

Weakly, Aprile collapsed on to the bed. 'You really intend to go through with it, then?' she.

gasped. 'Haven't you listened to a word I've said? Does it matter nothing to you that the chief qualification desired in a Sicilian bride is a capacity for hard work?'

Rosalba dared to tease her outraged cousin: 'I like hard work.' Then taking pity on her cousin's stricken look, she chided gently: 'It's you who haven't listened—if you had you would have heard me explain that marriage vows made under duress can't be considered binding.

'By marrying Salvatore I'll merely be pretending to carry out Grandfather's demands, but actually there'll be no commitment on either side. By this time tomorrow you and I might both be back home in England.' She sounded as surprised as she felt. 'Be prepared to make a dash for the airport the moment Salvatore is freed.'

Zia Giuseppina had arrived at the castle in a cart —according to Aprile, whose fastidious nose had wrinkled—one of the *carretti* used exclusively by the island peasants, with side and back panels painted with scenes of popular folklore such as the battles of the Paladins, incidents out of Ariosto, clashes between the Arabs and the Normans, and many other events plucked from the island's torrid past. Rosalba considered the cart's painted shafts and wheels to be works of art and had been astonished to learn that the intricate designs worked in wrought iron were all fashioned by hand. On feast days and special occasions, Salvatore had mentioned, the carthorse had many coloured feathers strapped on to his head and clusters of ribbons tied to the silver plate keeping the harness together in the middle of his back.

Brass bells, polished to resemble gold, jingled on various parts of the horse's body. She was not surprised, therefore, as Rita ushered Zia Giuseppina into her bedroom, to see that she had discarded her usual black in favour of a brightly-coloured skirt woven from native wool, a white chemise, and a fine lace shawl draped over her head and left to hang loosely around her shoulders.

She was standing in the middle of the room wondering what reaction to expect from the old woman who had unknowingly offered friendship to one of the hated Rossis. But Zia Giuseppina herself seemed full of purpose as, quite undaunted by her luxurious surroundings, she marched up to Rosalba and without a word of explanation ran her fingers through her silvery hair.

Surprised and puzzled, Rosalba obeyed when the old woman stepped slightly back and commanded: 'Give me your hand.' A golden ring was slid on to her finger, then a dainty lace-trimmed handkerchief pressed into her palm.

'This traditional custom ought to have been carried out during your betrothal ceremony,' Zia Giuseppina informed her with dignity, 'but as Toto made no mention of his plans and none of the usual signs was present to enable me to guess, I have been unable to carry out the duty until today. I shall, of course, take Toto to task for his secrecy,' her lips pursed. 'All that was needed was for him to present you with a gift of a red flower or a red ribbon to wear in your hair, then we would all have been aware of his intention. As it is, we have been taken completely by surprise. Word that his marriage was due to be solemnised today reached me late last evening—which is why I rose before the break of day in order to arrive in time for the ceremony. It is unthinkable that such important rites should be performed without the presence of at least one of his family. Tell me, child,' her eyes suddenly pinpointed Rosalba's face, sharp as needles, 'are you sure you care enough for my nephew to forgo all this?' Her wave encompassed the room padded with comfort. 'Are you strong enough to leave this feathered nest to live on a shelf in the mountains where cold winds blow? Toto will not forsake his people,' she stressed fiercely. 'And he will always be *capoccio*—head of his household, expecting complete subjection from his bride.'

Rosalba had neither the time nor the words to explain that she was marrying Salvatore simply to give him his freedom, so she had no choice but to prevaricate.

'I will do whatever is necessary to his happiness,' she whispered with complete truth.

Zia Giusepinna seemed satisfied. 'Then I will delay you no longer.' She stepped towards the door, then hesitated to cast a look almost of gratitude. 'Usually marriage is celebrated as a new beginning —yours will be doubly celebrated because it will bring to a close a bitter vendetta. Once Toto slides the ring on to your finger, *tutto finisce*—everything finishes! Don't be shy with your new husband, *cara* —a devil, after all, is merely a fallen angel. Cling fast to the bridal rein, and your white hands will lead him out of hell!'

At ten o'clock precisely Rosalba's grandfather ar-

rived to escort her to the church where her reluctant
bridegroom was waiting. He was striding purpose-
fully across the room towards her when she turned
to face him and at the sight of her he stopped dead,
his hard eyes softening as they raked a wand-slim
figure dressed for sacrifice in virginal lace, her pale,
angelic features framed in a cloud of tulle. That he
was reminded of a far-off day when his less hard-
ened heart had leapt at the sight of his own shy
young bride was obvious when in a husky, trembling voice, he complimented:

'*Cara*, you look adorable far too precious to be
wasted upon Diavolo.' The mention of Salvatore's
name seemed to act as a reminder. Shaking free of
memories, he offered her his arm. 'Come,' he
frowned, 'your bridegroom is not a patient man, it
would be most unwise to keep him waiting.'

The small church that for centuries had served
the family and villagers alike was tucked into a
corner of the grounds, mere yards from the castle.
It had been built during the Norman occupation,
an artistic masterpiece with a small dome and an
elegant bell tower with three orders of mullioned
windows. Inside were wonderful Byzantine mosaics
depicting hunting scenes; the chase and capture of
wild beasts struck Rosalba as symbolic when her
eyes swept the length of the short aisle and came to
rest upon her bridegroom pacing a square yard of
marble floor, looking caged, frustrated by invisible
shackles.

When, at her appearance, an organ began softly
playing, his head jerked upright and he stood in
frozen stillness as she progressed towards him, his

dark piercing glance driving the last vestige of colour from her cheeks.

If there were people present in the church she did not see them, if there were whispers she did not hear them. During the short, traumatic period of time while she knelt upon a red velvet cushion close to the altar rails and a solemn but kindly priest guided her through her responses, only she and Salvatore existed in a makebelieve world. She felt deathly cold, yet when he took her hand to slide his ring on to her finger flame shot through her at his touch, bells pealed, and a heavenly choir of voices soared in praise.

She was halfway down the aisle, gripping hard upon her husband's arm, by the time she realised that the ceremony was over and the sounds she could hear were real. Rosalba Rossi was no more, her place had been taken by Signora Diavolo, a woman whose face was frozen into an expression of serenity, whose heart seemed the only madly thumping part of her left alive.

As they walked from the gloom of the church outside into sunshine laughing children ran to scatter handfuls of rose petals at their feet while their cheering parents formed a guard of honour that stretched from the church to the steps leading up to the castle. Like an automaton, Rosalba turned before entering the castle to sketch a grateful wave of acknowledgement, hoping the smile she forced upon stiff lips reflected a bride's joy and happiness and betrayed none of the shocked dismay she was actually feeling.

'*The ceremony will be no more than a farce,*' she

had assured Aprile, 'neither of us need feel in the least committed.'

But she did feel committed, finally and irrevocably committed by her own hushed, solemnly spoken vows, and by Salvatore's stern yet determined responses. He had sounded like a man accepting penance for his sins, as if marriage to herself was an act of atonement whose severity he welcomed as the price of absolution.

Yet his first words to her when, for a moment, they stood alone in the great hall, showed that he was not altogether reconciled, that in a corner of his heart resentment still rankled. Taking her chin between forceful fingers, he examined her pale beauty, slowly, thoroughly, taking his time.

'Well, dear wife, will you prove to be fair exchange for freedom? The old snake showed an unflattering determination to be rid of you—but then to gain his own ends he would sell even his share of the sun.'

'I am not one of my grandfather's possessions!' She dared to combat his mean temper.

'No,' he agreed, displaying a certainty that froze her blood, 'the charm of ownership is entirely mine. Why then do I feel cheated? Is it because I have caught the vixen but been denied the pleasure of the chase?'

Not unnaturally, considering the opposing personalities seated around the table, their wedding breakfast was a strained affair. Aprile spoke little, contenting herself with directing glances of mute hostility towards Salvatore, who shrugged his indifference and directed all his attention upon his aunt who sat like a spectre at the feast, leaving every course all but untouched. The Conte, attempting an attitude of benevolent approval, chatted lightly as one rich, colourful dish after another was served. Sicilians are a tough race and their food accords with their character, yet eventually even the Conte fell silent, a victim of the tense, fraught atmosphere.

They ploughed their way through traditional dishes of the island; from Palermo, pasta with sardines with its aromatic blend of sea and woodland flavours, then mullet deliciously cooked in olive oil, lemon juice and parsley. For the meat course there was *involtini alla Siciliana*, thin slices of meat rolled and filled with salami, cheese, breadcrumbs and onion, and for dessert the famous *cassata*, a mixture of sponge cake, almond paste, chocolate, cinnamon and candied peel.

'Will you try a glass of Mamertino, *signora*?' the Conte extended courtesy to Zia Giuseppina. 'It is our foremost Sicilian wine, I think you will agree, old enough to have been praised by Caesar.'

'Thank you, no.' Zia Giuseppina's hand reached out to cover the top of her glass. 'Its flavour is too civilised for my palate, I prefer the wine of my own region—primitive, full-bodied and slightly bitter—which description, come to think of it, could equally apply to its people.'

It was the first time Rosalba had seen her grandfather disconcerted. He preferred to converse with sophisticates such as himself who possessed a great number of ready-made, acceptable opinions on the greatest number of topics; the old woman's absence of pretension had the unpleasant effect of making him feel ill at ease at his own table.

This fact could have accounted for the excess of hauteur in his voice when he directed Salvatore: 'My villa on the coast has been made ready for your honeymoon. You and Rosalba may stay there for as long as you wish. As soon as you are ready, I will direct Alessandro to drive you there in my limousine.'

Salvatore flung his napkin down on to the table with such force Rosalba was startled. 'No, Signor Conte, you will not!' He leant across the table to stress: 'My wife will travel where, when, and by whatever mode of transport *I* choose.'

Their eyes clashed, exchanging a look that was hostile, full of dislike. Salvatore was asserting unsought authority over his bride. The Conte was slow to delegate, yet the powerful Sicilian characteristic of *capoccio* was so ingrained that even he had to concede defeat to the head of the house of Diavolo.

But it was done without grace. Rosalba felt sickened when, churlish with hatred, her grandfather ground out his detestation of the younger man.

'You first infiltrated my home in the manner of a bat skulking through the shadows of darkness. I knew then that your presence was an ill omen; the peasantry are not far wrong in their superstitious assertion that the bat is an embodiment of the devil! Take good care of my granddaughter, Diavolo, for if one hair of her head is harmed I will take great pleasure in emulating the manner in which your friends despatch the creature they loathe. You'll be caught, killed, and nailed to a barn door with your limbs outspread!'

CHAPTER THIRTEEN

IT was hard to decide who was suffering the highest degree of outraged pride when the cart pulled away from the castle with Salvatore in the driving seat, Zia Giuseppina queening by his side, and Rosalba, as befitted her lowly station, sitting at the rear with her legs tucked under her.

Spots of bright red colour flared high in the Conte's cheeks as he stood at the top of the steps watching the cart meandering slowly down the drive. Aprile stood next to him with lips firmly buttoned to suppress opinions she had not had the chance to air. Desperately, under cover of making her goodbyes, she had condemned Rosalba: 'You promised that the ceremony would be the end of this farce. If you leave with him now you will be branded his possession and never allowed to leave Sicily!'

'I must carry on the pretence for just a little while longer,' Rosalba had urged her cousin to understand. 'Those two hate one another; I must be certain that Salvatore is well beyond Grandfather's reach before I return to England. Don't worry, Aprile, in a few more hours I'll be back.'

Nevertheless, she could not help feeling that Salvatore was deliberately goading her grandfather's temper. There was a glint of unmistakable satisfaction in his eyes when he mocked:

'Smile at your grandfather, *viso d'angelo*, assure him that you are happy, for he seems to suspect that you are being driven straight to hell!'

Angel face. The sarcastic endearment angered her. She settled as comfortably as she could in the corner of the cart, resigning herself to enduring a few last hours of discomfort before becoming finally rid of the tormenting devil.

Once out upon the open road the horse progressed at surprising speed, clip-clopping down the mountain road with an hypnotic rhythm that set her head nodding. For the past three days her mind had been in such turmoil she had not slept; assured that the worst was now over, she curled into a ball and fell asleep.

It must have been a couple of hours later when she was jolted awake. The cart had stopped at a fork in the road. Through dazed eyes she saw Salvatore bend to kiss his aunt's cheek before he handed over the reins and jumped down from the driving seat.

'Come along, sleepyhead!' He strode round and in one easy movement lifted her from the cart.

'Where are we going?' Her voice was so sleepy, her yawn so defenceless, he grinned.

'On our honeymoon, child bride, where else? Say goodbye to Zia Giuseppina, this is where we part company, we'll travel the rest of the way by jeep.'

He seemed in no hurry to put her down. Of necessity she had slung one arm around his neck when he had lifted her from the cart, an unthinking gesture that had now taken on an aura of unbearable intimacy. His face was so close his breath brushed her cheek, warm and gentle as a kiss. As she stared up at him he bent closer, his smile fading as he gazed long and deeply into violet, sleep-drugged depths that seemed to hold his mesmerised attention.

Sensing Zia Giuseppina's amused glance, Rosalba twisted out of his grasp until her feet touched the ground, then stepped back a pace, panting with exertion, devastated by the effect his merest touch had upon her senses.

The jeep had been left where two roads met and as they climbed into it his aunt edged her horse along a track leading up towards her village. As she jogged past she leant sideways to cackle:

'Enjoy your honeymoon, children! Stay angry with each other, for the anger of lovers renews their love!'

Without response, Salvatore started up the jeep and drove—as Rosalba mentally termed it—like a bat out of hell, so that she was bounced unmercifully and had to grip hard upon the upholstery in order to keep her seat. Speech was impossible. Even when he turned off the side road and on to a main highway he continued driving as if possessed, for hour after silent hour, putting the width of the island between herself and the castle where Aprile would be vainly waiting.

It was early evening by the time their hurtling progress eased enough to allow her glimpses of sea lapping sandy beaches with, in the background, an enormous mountain mass towering thousands of feet above and sweeping majestically down to meet the waters. She did not need to be told that it was Etna, the huge isolated mountain whose slopes were so often menaced by the anger of a very active volcano.

She glimpsed villages and cultivated land on the lower slopes and beyond them a grey charred area that reminded her of a desert of ashes bearing not a trace of vegetation. Still higher was a chaos of smoking rocks, burning soil out of which welled sulphuric fumes. At the peak was a crater wreathed in smoke from which streams of lava trickled like saliva from a gaping mouth. She dreaded the thought of approaching nearer, and was vastly relieved when Salvatore turned the jeep in the direction of the coast.

Stars were glittering bright in a black sky when finally he drew the jeep to a halt. She could smell and hear the nearby sea surging in on a whispering flurry of foam that reached almost to a square-built building looming out of the darkness. She realised that it was situated on the edge of a bay when lights from a scattering of fishing boats began twinkling like fireflies upon the water.

She stepped from the jeep and stumbled through soft sand in his wake. A key turned in a lock, a light switch clicked, then he ushered her into a beach apartment, sparsely furnished with only the bare necessities required of a holiday home—built-in wardrobe; a bed with shelves either side holding books and a lamp; cool tiled floor, and two tiny rooms leading off from the main one—a kitchen and a bathroom.

'It has been lent to us by a friend of mine,' he intruded into her stunned silence. 'Less luxurious than your grandfather's villa, I dare say, but adequate for our needs.'

'You mean we're to spend the night here?' she jerked.

'A night, a week, a month?' he shrugged, 'who knows? It depends entirely upon the depths of our absorption in each other.'

Rosalba drew in a deep, steadying breath. 'Salvatore, for days I've been trying to explain something to you, but each time you've refused to listen. Will you please hear me out *now*?'

He swung on his heel and walked in the direction of the kitchen. 'At the moment I am too hungry to pay attention to idle chatter. There's no hurry, whatever you wish to discuss can wait until after we've eaten.'

It could not. Even a short delay would make it all the more difficult to find alternative accommodation so late at night. But as nervously she stepped past the double bed dominating the single apartment, she wisely decided to delay her argument. One could not reason with a man made ravenous with hunger, much better to wait until he was in a calm, receptive mood.

She felt shy at first of rubbing shoulders with him in the compact kitchen into which had been crammed a small but modern cooker, a sink, a cupboard stacked with dishes and provisions, and a bench-type seat with a strip of table combined that was attached to the one clear wall.

'How do you like your omelettes?' he quizzed, an upraised eyebrow causing her heart to flutter. 'Runny or well done?'

'Runny, of course ...' she replied absently, fully occupied in keeping a rein on racing pulses.

'Good.' He reached for a pan, tossing the dry observation across his shoulder: 'It bodes well for our marriage—discovering that we have at least one thing in common.'

They were certainly not emotionally compatible, she decided, as with trembling fingers she set two places on the strip of table. Salvatore seemed nerveless, calm to the point of aloofness, as he shared the omelette between two plates, slid next to her on the bench, and began steadily to eat.

When she transferred the first forkful to her mouth the fluffy concoction almost choked her. It tasted delicious, its consistency just right, yet when she tried to swallow her throat clamped tight around a substance that seemed suddenly to have turned into rubber.

'Bread ...?' He pushed the bread basket and butter dish in front of her.

'No ... thank you,' she choked.

'Wine, then ...' He poured a generous amount of Corvo into two glasses, downed his own in a couple of gulps, then immediately refilled it.

He had finished his huge portion of omelette and had pushed away his plate with a replete sigh before he noticed that her meal was congealing on her plate, her wine had been left untouched in her glass.

'What's this?' His jeering tone took her by surprise. 'First night nerves? Surely not! Since you have had the advantage of a dress rehearsal, tonight must offer few surprises.'

'That's what I want to talk to you about,' she stumbled. Then haste spurred her tongue. 'For days I've been trying——'

'Let's move out of here.' He stretched, irked by constricted elbows. Casually he lighted a cheroot, stood up, and strolled into the other room.

Anger such as she had never before experienced sent her erupting after him. 'Aren't you *ever* going to listen to me?'

Her raw-nerved retort sent him spinning round to face her. 'So,' he eyed the spitting ball of fury, 'Mona Lisa is possessed of a temper!'

Courage drained out of her as he towered, darkly intimidating in the outfit his aunt had brought for him to wear at his wedding—slim black pants tucked inside knee-high riding boots that had the dense shine of ebony; black shirt, unbuttoned to the waist to expose a *porta fortuna* medallion tangled within dark hairs matted across a broad, tanned chest. Aprile was right, he had more than his fair share of masculinity; *machismo* flowed from him, barbaric as the golden buckle holding the belt around his waist—the buckle depicting a beast and a reptile from which she was finding it impossible to raise her eyes.

'Repose marks your caste, remember, *cara*. I will overlook your minor lapse—proceed with whatever it is you wish to tell me.'

'It's to do with the night we spent together in the cave ... the night you ... you ...'

'Don't be ashamed to speak of it,' his tone was cool. 'Despite our intensely rigid code of morals, clandestine sexual intercourse is no rarity in Sicily. Only some seventy-five per cent of our girls are virgins when they marry, indeed, some village priests maintain that immorality is rife and demand proof of virginity after the wedding night. Many a cockerel has been slain by the mothers of newly-wed girls in order to display linen stained with blood, and many a confessional shares the secrets of mothers shamed into pulling the wool over the eyes of a priest.'

Suspecting that he had set out cruelly and deliberately to intensify her embarrassment, Rosalba whipped up sufficient courage to meet fire with fire.

'You didn't seduce me, you passed out because I'd dosed your drink with sleeping pills!'

Her words dropped like stones, one by one, into a void that stretched into a fraught, dangerous silence.

'You did *what*?' The cheroot fell from his fingers and was ground to ashes beneath a savage heel. Full of pent-up menace, his eyes pinning, daring her to move, he advanced closer. 'Have you the gall to admit that you manoeuvred me into falling for the oldest trick known to womankind? That I have forsaken my freedom for the sake of a non-existent child?' Impelled by anger beyond his control, he grabbed her shoulders and shook her hard. '*Why*, in the name of God, *why* . . .?'

'In order to save your life,' she babbled, half crazed with fear, 'to put an end to a stupid vendetta that has already cost too many lives!'

'*Tu sei davvero una cane!*' He flung her with a force that sent her sprawling across the bed. 'No wife of mine interferes in the affairs of men!'

'I'm not your wife,' she gasped. 'No court in the world will hold us to vows that were forced upon us! I intend returning home as soon as I'm able, once I'm gone you can forget I ever existed.'

When he leant forward she shrank from his sibilant hiss. 'I struck a bargain with your grandfather—a hospital in exchange for making you my bride. But a hospital is useless without money to run it. If the welfare of my people is dependent upon your having a child *then a child you shall have!*'

It seemed to her that when he snapped off the light the room was filled with the glare from eyes holding beacons of flame as he bore down upon her. She struggled to escape, but was too late to avoid a volcanic eruption that heaped heat and pain, terror and tears upon her defenceless body. The room heaved, his breath roared in her ear, his hands traced a searing, lava-hot trail that scarred, scorched and shrivelled every untouched, flawless part of her.

He seemed deaf to moans of pain, a devil bent upon dragging her down into his hell. Yet it was not quite hell. In time, it seemed, she became suspended in a sort of limbo, the fringe of hell, that region assigned to tormented souls to whom, through no fault of their own, the benefits of redemption did not apply—a limbo large and broad that some intuitive poet had once labelled 'the paradise of fools'.

Hours later she sidled from his side, leaving him still wrapped in black-browed sleep, and crept outside to watch the sun rise. She felt numbed, yet every part of her ached with pain. He had not been kind, as she felt sure it was in his nature to be kind. He had taken her in the manner of an animal whose sole aim is the continuation of his species. There had been no softly-murmured words of love, no tenderness in the hands that had forced upon her the sort of intimacy all girls dwell upon during their nubile years but to which she, in her innocence, had given no more than a passing thought. Marriage, when she had considered it, had appealed more as a state of companionship, the setting up of a home with a man prepared to cosset and protect. The begetting of children had remained a mystical rite fancifully bound up with the legend of Aphrodite, the goddess of a heather-clad mountain whose association with bees and honey was legendary, as was the belief of great antiquity that winds off the heather were responsible for the impregnation of women.

Stifling an hysterical inclination to laugh and scream at one and the same time, Rosalba held on to sanity yet could not suppress a surge of resentment against parents who had kept her isolated as a princess locked up in an ivory tower.

She sat down on a flat rock to ease her weary limbs and gazed with unseeing eyes at a wreath of pearly grey mist dispersing from the peak of the volcano that only yesterday had filled her with dread and which she could now regard with complete indifference. Her head bowed—a flower wilted by a storm of violence—oblivious of the fiery sun rising swiftly out of the horizon, of fields, hills and buildings tinged with gold, of the sea shining like polished silver.

When a shadow fell across her face she stiffened but had no need to look up—her senses were so sensitive to his presence that even the touch of his shadow set raw nerves leaping.

'Why didn't you tell me that you were a virgin?' His voice sounded strained, his face as she would have seen immediately had she bothered to look up was scored with lines of deep anxiety.

'You never listened to anything I tried to say. Besides,' her tone was lack-lustre, 'would it have made any difference?'

He reached out a hand as if compelled to stroke silver strands of hair that looked too heavy for a drooping head, but after momentary hesitation it was withdrawn.

'Probably not,' the confession grated from his lips. 'Deep inside I think I've always known.'

He had hurt her deeply, yet still she could not bear to hear the agony of self-condemnation in his voice. She looked up and saw a face haggard with regret, his mouth a bitter twist, his eyes alive with a furnace of frustration. As tensely he braced for her condemnation, expecting words of understandable hatred, a white dove fluttered past, settled upon a flowering creeper, and began to coo. The soft sound acted like balm upon a sting as the fraught silence was filled with the delightful sound of a lovebird calling his mate.

As if sensing that the message had touched her heart, Salvatore approached cautiously, swallowing hard to disperse an unaccustomed taste of humility.

'May I sit with you?'

Rosalba tensed as if to flee, mistrustful of the diffident stranger, then with a sigh she shrugged her indifference, her eyes mirroring a hopeless dejection that caused him to wince.

He sat as close as he dared without actually touch-

ing and quietly began to speak. At first his flat
monotone made little sense, her mind was too numb
to react, but gradually she began to sense that behind his terse, disjointed sentences lay a message
which, unbelievably, he was too uncertain of himself to spell out.

'Often I find myself wondering why this lovely
island of ours should be cursed with heartrending
poverty. It has been blessed with plentiful amounts
of minerals and sulphur, its climate is ideal for the
cultivation of fruit, vegetables and crops of every
description. Bananas, grapes, cotton, grow in abundance and the soil is so fertile and well irrigated it is
possible to harvest several crops a year. Yet the
peasants receive trifling wages and live in the most
sordid conditions. Basically, my country is in need
not only of capital and industry but also of leaders
to guide its people out of the past and educate them
in the modern methods of agriculture, instead of
allowing them to follow the example of their cousins
and brothers who emigrated to America, Canada
and other such countries where they are now making their fortunes producing fruit and wine in
climates similar to our own.'

Slowly, wary of alarming her timidity, he reached
out a hand and touched her cheek, turning her head
so that she was forced to look at him. Holding puzzled blue eyes with his own dark gaze, he grated: 'I
can never leave here, Rosalba, I am destined to stay
with those who most need my help. In any other
country I could prosper, my wife and children
would enjoy the benefits of the high living standards
accepted as normal by the people of more enlight-

ened nations, whereas here,' his bitter tone revived, 'I can promise little in the way of material benefits ...'

A small bird of happiness caged deep within her began struggling for release. Her eyes pleaded with him to be sincere when, feeling wings fluttering madly in her throat, she breathed a diffident reply.

'Riches are not anything like so important as ...'

'As what ...?' he urged, suddenly very close, very eager. Confusion swept her when she felt his arm enclosing her waist, the grip of his fingers betraying the agony of tightly-held control. 'Were you about to say *love*, Rosalba?' he breathed against her ear. 'That, *cara*, is something I can offer you in abundance. *Tesoro mio! Io ti amo ...!*'

Completely unnerved by the ravaged, harshly uttered words of love, she collapsed against him and was swept hard against his chest. 'Generous, forgiving heart,' he murmured, shaken to the depths by her surrender, '*ti adoro!*'

His kiss was an exercise in discipline that lifted her on a gentle tide of cosseting, making her feel nursed in caring, loving arms. For a while she luxuriated in his solicitude, but then, perversely feminine, she decided that, though water was good for quenching thirst, she preferred intoxicating champagne. He was deliberately holding back, afraid of frightening her, so, as his passion was so tightly bottled, she dared to pop the cork.

Wantonly wicked, she moved against him, parting her soft lips in sensuous invitation, putting into practice the expertise she had learned only a few hours before, arousing the somnolent tiger so that words growled in his throat.

'*Tormenting vixen* ...!' With a blaze in his eyes that she found satisfying, he swept her off her feet and began striding towards the apartment. Earth and sky revolved, steadying just long enough to allow her a glimpse of a benign Etna before he kicked open the door and whisked her inside. As he laid her on the bed she smiled a secret smile. Like Etna, her volcanic husband would not always be dormant, often he would erupt, but like those who dared to live on volcanic slopes she would learn to gauge moods, to sense when it was wise to run and when it was safe to stay.

Already intuition was at work, warning her that at that very moment it would be most unwise of her to run—and heaven to remain.

The bestselling epic saga of the Irish. An intriguing and passionate story that spans 400 years.

FIRST...

The Defiant

Lady Elizabeth Hatton, highborn Englishwoman, was not above using her position to get what she wanted ...and more than anything in the world she wanted Rory O'Donnell, the fiery Irish rebel. But it was an alliance that promised only ruin....

THEN...

The Survivors

Against a turbulent background of political intrigue and royal corruption, the determined, passionate Shanna O'Hara searched for peace in her beloved but troubled Ireland. Meanwhile in England, hot-tempered Brenna Coke fought against a loveless marriage....

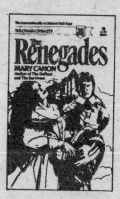
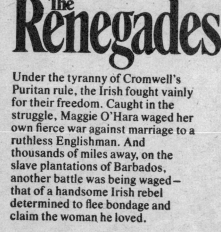

Take these
best-selling
4 novels
FREE

That's right! FOUR first-rate Harlequin romance novels by four world renowned authors, FREE, as your introduction to the Harlequin Presents Subscription Plan. Be swept along by these FOUR exciting, poignant and sophisticated novels . . . . Travel to the Mediterranean island of Cyprus in **Anne Hampson**'s "Gates of Steel" . . . to Portugal for **Anne Mather**'s "Sweet Revenge" . . . to France and **Violet Winspear**'s "Devil in a Silver Room" . . . and the sprawling state of Texas for **Janet Dailey**'s "No Quarter Asked."

Harlequin Presents...

The very finest in romantic fiction

Join the millions of avid Harlequin readers all over the world who delight in the magic of a really exciting novel. EIGHT great NEW titles published EACH MONTH! Each month you will get to know exciting, interesting, true-to-life people . . . . You'll be swept to distant lands you've dreamed of visiting . . . . Intrigue, adventure, romance, and the destiny of many lives will thrill you through each Harlequin Presents novel.

Get all the latest books before they're sold out!

As a Harlequin subscriber you actually receive your personal copies of the latest Presents novels immediately after they come off the press, so you're sure of getting all 8 each month.

Cancel your subscription whenever you wish!

You don't have to buy any minimum number of books. Whenever you decide to stop your subscription just let us know and we'll cancel all further shipments.

Your FREE gift *includes*

Sweet Revenge by **Anne Mather**
Devil in a Silver Room by **Violet Winspear**
Gates of Steel by **Anne Hampson**
No Quarter Asked by **Janet Dailey**

FREE Gift Certificate
and subscription reservation

Mail this coupon today!

In the U.S.A.
1440 South Priest Drive
Tempe, AZ 85281

In Canada
649 Ontario Street
Stratford, Ontario N5A 6W2

Harlequin Reader Service:

Please send me my 4 Harlequin Presents books free. Also, reserve a subscription to the 8 new Harlequin Presents novels published each month. Each month I will receive 8 new Presents novels at the low price of $1.75 each [*Total — $14.00 a month*]. There are no shipping and handling or any other hidden charges. I am free to cancel at any time, but even if I do, these first 4 books are still mine to keep absolutely FREE without any obligation.

NAME _____ (PLEASE PRINT)

ADDRESS _____ (APT. NO.)

CITY _____ STATE / PROV. ___ ZIP / POSTAL CODE

Offer expires March 31, 1983
Offer not valid to present subscribers

SB532

If price changes are necessary, you will be notified.